THEIRS IS THE KINGDOM

THE WESTMINSTER PRESS · PHILADELPHIA

Theirs
Is the Kingdom

By JACK M. MacLEOD

ILLUSTRATED BY PAUL V. LANTZ

Printed in the United States of America

CONTENTS

THIS BOOK . . .

brings you a series of exciting pictures of the kinds of things that have happened to Christian people in the long years since the church of Jesus Christ began. Only here and there in it will you find the names of famous men or familiar events. But what the stories tell of how the church and its people grew and changed is true, *even though it is* fiction.

Although the main characters in the book are imaginary, real people took chances like this and suffered like this. Without them we would not have the church as we know it now. Their names may be forgotten, but God remembers them well. And Jesus said about such people,

"Blessed are the poor in spirit,

for **THEIRS IS THE KINGDOM** *of heaven."*

NOTE: On pages 223 and 224 you can discover where each story was supposed to take place, what the facts are in each chapter, and how to pronounce the names of the people and places mentioned.

The Owl and the Cup

MANAHEN WORKED to get the wrappings off the small box. Four men huddled around him, their shadows looming on the walls. Outside, the night was black over the ancient city of Antioch.

7

A few moments before, somebody had startled them by rattling on the iron gate of the courtyard. When they went out to see, they found the package stuck in the gate. It had Manahen's name on it.

Now Manahen was lifting the top off the box. He straightened up. There in the box, a dead owl stared up at him.

"Brethren," he whispered, "you are in danger because of me. I must leave at once."

They looked up at him. Barnabas began to say something, but Manahen held up his hand. "This owl is a sign of death," he said. "The owl—he lives among the tombs."

"Oh, now—" Barnabas said.

"No, I am right," Manahen went on. "This owl is the sign of death! It comes from King Agrippa. He means it! Several years ago he ruined Herod Antipas, my foster brother. Now he has found me. This house is not a safe place for any of you."

Paul went over to the cupboard and brought back a loaf of bread and the Lord's cup. "I don't know about that owl," he said, "but here is the sign of Jesus Christ. Who is stronger, our divine Lord or Herod Agrippa?"

Simeon and Barnabas nodded their heads.

"Perhaps the owl *is* a sign of death for you, Manahen," Paul went on. "If it is, we will share it with you, all of us together. We share the sign and seal of life together in our Lord's Holy Supper. Death

8

cannot make us afraid." He filled the cup and broke the bread in pieces. Each of them around the table took one of the pieces.

"My brothers," Manahen said, "you make my heart glad. I thank the Lord Jesus, for he has allowed me to be part of this family of love and faith."

They ate the bread and passed the cup around the table. Then they prayed together.

In a few moments Manahen stood up. "Now, brethren," he said, "I must go. If our Lord wills, perhaps I shall see you again. God be with you."

He put the top back on the box and picked it up. But as he turned to go, Paul caught his arm. "Elder brother," he said, "if you are really going out to meet death tonight, let me come with you."

Manahen looked at him. He smiled. "You do my heart good, Paul. Do come with me. Good-by, my friends."

The two men went out into the courtyard and slipped through the gate. The narrow street was black and empty.

They had not gone far before they heard someone following them. They hurried faster and soon reached a large square. They stepped quickly into an alley between two buildings. In a moment, a man passed by.

"He won't go far that way," Manahen whispered. "Soon he will see that we've slipped away from him. Hurry!"

They headed for the road that would take them
west along the river toward the sea. Several miles
farther they came to a low bluff overlooking their
path. They went up to the bluff's grassy rim, where
they could watch the trail without being seen. In a
few moments, they saw their tracker pass by along
the riverbank. He disappeared around a bend.

"Who is he?" Paul whispered.

"I don't know," Manahen answered. "But he is a servant of King Agrippa."

Paul frowned. "Why would the king send you an owl?"

Manahen sighed deeply. "Agrippa uses the owl as a sign when he is out to get revenge. He has always hated his family, and with good cause. When he was three years old, his father was murdered by his grandfather." Paul nodded his head. "But the owl," Manahan went on, "came in seven years ago, when Tiberius threw him into prison. Agrippa was standing under a tree in chains. An old German slave saw an owl perched over his head. He hobbled over and told him it was a sign that Agrippa would soon be free; and truly, in six months Tiberius died. The new emperor was Agrippa's good friend. He set him free and gave him a chain of gold for his chains of iron."

The two men were silent for a while. The breeze whispered through the trees along the riverbank. The moon had risen in the night sky.

At last Manahen said: "You know, it's a wonder Agrippa hasn't tracked me down before now. Perhaps he found out about me from our brethren in Jerusalem."

"Oh, no," Paul answered. "They would never tell him!"

Manahen sighed. "Agrippa's spies are very crafty. You saw this one tonight. Why, only the best spy could have followed us through Antioch in the dark. He might be watching us right now!" He rose to his feet. "Come. We must get to the coast before dawn."

"To Seleucia?" gasped Paul. "You are not—"

"Yes," said Manahen. "I am going to get a ship for Caesarea. I must face Agrippa. Then perhaps he will take out his anger on me and leave the church alone."

Paul stood up quickly. He followed Manahen down the path around the bluff.

"But that's certain death, elder brother!"

"Does it matter?" Manahen asked. "No, I want to take this owl back to Agrippa. If I should lose my life now, it would be only a small gift to Christ. But it is a willing gift for the sake of his church. You would not keep me from doing this."

In the morning the two men got to the seaport. Soon they found a small coastal ship about to set sail for the south.

Paul stood back under a shed, ready to wave a last farewell to Manahen. The ship had begun to push off from the great wharf, when their tracker dashed out of an alley. He jumped onto the deck of the ship and ran toward Manahen, a knife held high. But before he could stab Manahen, a sailor saw the blade flash. He pounced on him and knocked him down. Very quickly he grabbed the man's wrist and twisted; the knife clattered to the deck.

Soon the small ship sailed out into the open sea.

The captain ordered the stranger dragged to him on the afterdeck.

"Keep quiet!" ordered the captain, as the man tried to speak. He read the short scroll which the sailor had taken from the man's pouch. "So," he said, "your name is Sacar. You serve King Agrippa. What brings you aboard my ship with a dagger waving in the air?"

"Let me loose and put this traitor under arrest!" Sacar demanded. He pointed at Manahen.

"Who are you, sir? What is your crime?" asked the captain of Manahen.

Manahen held out his hand and showed the captain his ring. It had the royal crest of the Herod family engraved on it. "I was once an adviser to Herod Antipas, sir—that is my crime."

"Arrest him, I say!" cried Sacar. "I will not allow him to escape! In the name of Agrippa, King of —"

"Silence!" ordered the captain sternly. "No man dares to give me orders on my own ship. I'm the master here." He motioned to the sailor. "Turn him loose. And if I have any trouble with you, bitter-face, I'll have you thrown overboard as bait for the sharks!"

Sacar glared at him but held his tongue.

"Now get down on the main deck, both of you," ordered the captain. "I warn you again, I will toss you both over the side if you give us any trouble."

13

Before long they reached the open sea. The ship
headed south along the Syrian coast. The day was
bright, without a cloud in the sky. A brisk ocean
breeze blew from the north. The small ship bucked
up the waves and flew down into the troughs.

    All day long the wind blew harder and harder. The sky filled with black clouds from horizon to horizon. The ship lifted and smashed through the heavy seas. The mainsail had been furled. A canvas sea anchor dragged on a heavy hemp line from the stern to keep the ship facing into the storm. The sailors dumped more and more cargo overboard. Huge waves towered over the small craft. Rain and scud whipped across the deck.

Sometime during the following night the line holding the sea anchor broke. With great difficulty the captain got the ship turned about. He had no choice then. The ship ran before the storm.

Daybreak came. The lookout could see only a little way across the crests of the great rolling swells. Suddenly he cried out. He waved his arms and pointed. The ship was headed right toward the shore!

Manahen stood clutching an iron ring in the bulkhead at his back. He could see through the driving rain the faint outline of land looming off the port bow. There was no mistaking what would happen. The storm would drive the ship onto the rocks. They would be smashed to bits in the pounding, giant breakers along the shore. Fear crept into his heart. He had a terrible feeling that he should not have come. Perhaps it had not been the will of God that he should see Agrippa. Surely, the end was coming!

"O God," he prayed, "forgive me if I have acted blindly or hastily. Remember not my sin! Help us, O Jesus. Bless these seamen. Receive our souls. . . ."

The vessel shot forward on the surging, driving seas. It was like a living creature leaping at the lash. Closer and closer it drove toward the looming cliffs.

Manahen went on praying. He remembered the love of his brethren in Christ. Slowly, his heart quieted. And he thought, Now, in a few more minutes, I will see the Lord face to face! I will be with him! He was no longer afraid, although the crash of the surf was like thunder.

He noticed that Sacar, his enemy, was standing near him. He was trying hard to keep on his feet. His face was white with panic. Manahen reached out to put his arm around his shoulders. With the fury of a wild animal, the man pushed away from Manahen's grasp. He stumbled two steps and fell on the deck. On hands and knees he scrambled to the railing and held on so tightly that his fingernails tore into the wood.

By now the ship was very close to the shore, almost under a great cliff. It drove forward on the boiling seas. Huge waves crashed down over the stern. Torrents of sea water sluiced down along the deck. Sacar lost his grip and disappeared. The ship rose high up on a mountain of water. It balanced at the top for a shuddering instant. Then, suddenly, it plunged down sickeningly into empty space. It capsized with a splintering, twisting crash. Tons of churning water rolled over it.

Manahen could feel himself being driven far down into the depths of the ocean. It seemed he would be torn to bits. He rolled on and on in the wild currents.

Some time later he found himself choking and gasping on his hands and knees in shallow water. He lurched to his feet and stumbled forward until he was out of the water, then fell down on the wet sand.

Manahen woke up. The sun was streaming in through a window. He was lying on a cot in a fisherman's hut. Only a few others from the ship had been found by the people of the small fishing village. Sacar, he learned, was not among the survivors.

After a week he was strong enough to start on his journey once more. One of the fishing boats took him to the next seaport along the coast. There he boarded a large ship going south. Two days later, at sunset, the ship passed the tower and entered the large harbor of Caesarea.

Many passengers left the ship, for a great festival was being held in Caesarea to honor the emperor. The city was crowded. Visitors had come from the whole province of Syria and from all over the Empire. Syrians and Jews wandered the streets. There were Greeks and Egyptians, Romans and Africans, princes, merchants, thieves, and beggars mingled in the crowds.

Finally Manahen found some Christians in a small net shop on the water front. That night they took him to their secret meeting place. Joyfully they worshiped God together. Far into the night they sang hymns and talked about the things of Christ.

Early the next morning Manahen went with his friends to the royal amphitheater, where King Agrippa was to make a speech of welcome. Manahen climbed high up on the side of the hill, where the crowds were not so great. He sat down to watch.

A military guard in shining armor marched into the theater. Behind them came a procession of drums. Two officers in plumed helmets marched in carrying standards bearing the Roman eagle and the image of the emperor. A great roar of applause swelled up from the large audience, who had risen to their feet.

Suddenly, in the midst of the shouting, there was a single blast from a trumpet. A glittering flash, as of the sun itself, appeared out of nowhere on the stage.

Then the people saw that it was King Agrippa! He was wearing a wonderful robe woven of shining silver thread. The early morning sunlight made it glitter and flash. "A god! A god!" the people cried. "He is a god, not a man!" The whole crowd took up the cry: "A god! A god!" The amphitheater was filled with shouting and cheering. King Agrippa smiled. Then he raised his hands.

"Citizens of Rome," he began, "thank you for your cheering. I welcome you to Caesarea and my kingdom of Judea. We gather here to honor Caesar, divine

god of Imperial Rome!" The crowd cheered once more. "To him we pledge our undying loyalty! We promise here to dedicate our lives to Rome—"

He stopped suddenly. He staggered back, clutching his chest, and doubled over in pain. The audience rose to their feet with a gasp. The men on the platform ran to him. In a moment he straightened up a little. He staggered to the front of the platform. The people leaned forward, instantly silent, to hear what he would say.

"My friends," Agrippa was speaking through clenched teeth, "you have called me a god. But I am going to die. Gods don't die!" He could not go on. The pain became violent. In great agony he fell to the ground. A squad of soldiers hurried to the platform. While the audience stood watching, they carried the king away.

Within an hour the story had spread everywhere through the city. Manahen wanted to go right to Agrippa's side. He had come to Caesarea just for this. By God's providence, even Sacar and a shipwreck had not stopped him. But now, if the king died, he would be free, and the church would not be attacked any more. He would be able to return to his Christian brethren in Antioch, there to serve the church through the last years of his life.

His Christian friends urged him to stay in hiding. All afternoon he struggled in prayer to find out the will of God. This time he dared not be hasty.

That night he tossed on his bed, unable to sleep.

21

He dressed and walked up into the hills overlooking the harbor and the ocean. For hours he knelt in prayer under a tree in the moonlight. Finally his mind grew calm; his heart was at peace. The night was very quiet, but in the quiet he seemed to hear Jesus speaking to him—*Agrippa needs you. Agrippa needs you. That is all that matters now.*

The next morning Manahen went to the royal palace. Through a large crowd of people he approached the palace gates. When the guards saw his ring they let him pass through. He entered a great marble hall and went up a long flight of stairs.

When he stepped into the royal bedchamber he found the king lying on his couch in great pain. Two physicians stood silently nearby.

"Manahen—" the king whispered in surprise.

"Yes," Manahen replied. "I come to you—in the name of Jesus, and by the providence of God. I came to give you back that owl you sent me in Antioch, but I lost it. I'm sorry you are so ill." He pulled a chair over next to the couch and sat down. He put his hand gently on Agrippa's arm. "Do you remember," he said quietly, "many years ago when you were

22

just a little boy? I used to carry you on my shoulders around the garden. And that horse I had—Prince Black—do you remember him? You used to ride behind the saddle. We would ride out across the dunes, and you would shout yourself hoarse. . . ."

Manahen went on talking quietly of the years long ago. At last he said: "Bitterness can make us forget those days, Agrippa. May the Lord Jesus not be too harsh with you. He knows every man's heart. He knows all the sore and bleeding wounds. May he forgive your sins, Agrippa, as he has mine. Have courage. He won't be long in coming now. . . ."

In a few days the king was dead. Manahen's Christian friends were no longer afraid. They wept as Manahen blessed them in the name of Jesus and said good-by.

Later Manahen stood at the prow of the northbound ship that would take him home to Antioch. He waved to the brethren on the beach. Then the ship weighed anchor, and sailed out of the harbor toward open water. The fresh sea breeze felt clean and good. A joyful escort of sea gulls screamed and cried in the air, swooping and swirling around the boat.

Manahen smiled as he watched them. The Herods were dead and gone from his life. He was on his way back to his true family—to Paul and Barnabas and Simeon Niger and all the good people of the church in Antioch. He lifted up his eyes and gave humble thanks to his Lord. He was going home!

The Fish of Galilee

B<small>UT</small>, V<small>ALERIAN</small>, they say he throws men to the fish!" whispered the scrawny, trembling galley slave. The cords of his neck stood out as he clenched his teeth in wide-eyed fear.

"You worry too much," said Valerian. "You wouldn't make good bait for a school of minnows!"

From the wharf came a sharp command. Then a man appeared on deck, followed respectfully by the galley captain. This was the great Admiral Maxentius, Imperial Commander of the Corinthian Gulfs. He was a small man, but his very name had struck terror into the hearts of the pirates of the Aegean Sea. He pointed four times toward the lines of oarsmen chained to their benches in the open hold. The galley overseer and a soldier came down the gangway and knocked the chains off the ankles of the four chosen slaves.

Valerian was the last. When his legs were free he stood up and snapped his wrist chains with a simple twist, for his arms were like bands of steel. Three years on the galley oars had made him hard and strong. He sneered in the overseer's face and tossed the chains over the side.

"Fish bait!" snarled the overseer.

Valerian turned and gazed down at his oarmate.

24

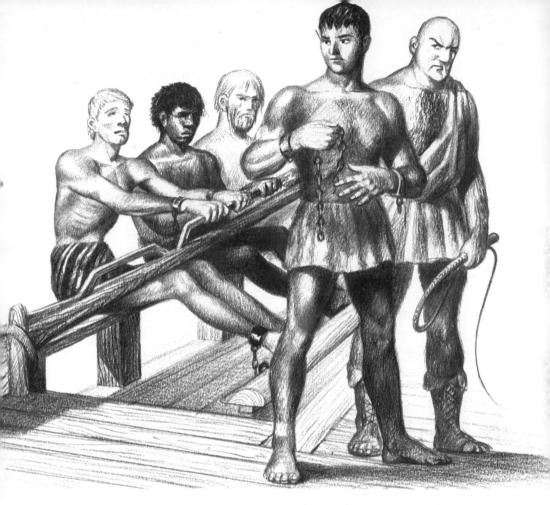

"Maybe you'll last another month," he said merci-
lessly. "Better than being crucified, isn't it, pirate!"

The slave looked up fearfully. "Good-by, Valerian," he moaned. But the only answer he got was the
cutting lash of the furious overseer. Valerian threw
back his head and laughed as he went down the gangway after the three other chosen slaves.

Valerian heard the slave bell ring. He went on sorting onions.

"Pig of a slave!" shouted the kitchen steward. "Will you ever learn? Go serve the master!"

Valerian let an onion slip out of his fingers and walked to the stone stairs leading up to the terrace.

"Turn and bow to me," roared the steward, his flabby face purple with rage, "or I'll see you're sent back to the galleys where you belong!"

Without a word Valerian went on up the steps. On the terrace his master sat writing at a table by the marble railing. A breeze stirred the gray wisps of hair on his balding head.

"You rang, sir," Valerian said.

The admiral grunted and went on writing. Valerian stood in the warm morning sunlight, watching him. I could snap his neck with two fingers, he thought. I could pick him up with one hand and throw him over the railing. The great Maxentius!

"Can you read or write, Valerian?" he asked.

"No, master."

The admiral looked up. His eyes were gentle, the color of the cloudless sky on a hazy day. He studied Valerian for a moment.

"You stand straight," he said. "You have an intelligent face. Three years in the galleys didn't break your spirit, I see." He turned away and gazed out over the city of Corinth sprawled below. "Tell me about yourself."

"There is little to tell, master. My family were Aegean islanders."

"Your father?"

"A shipmaster."

"You mean, a pirate," replied his master quietly.

"No, my lord," Valerian said. He looked down. His anger showed only in the reddening of his face. "My father was lost off the northern coast of Crete. His ship was sunk with a full cargo. His Roman creditors sold me into slavery to pay part of the debt."

"I see," said the admiral. He pushed back his chair and stood up. "You have served three months in the kitchen," he went on. "Now it is time for the next step. You will be taught to read and write. For now, you will be my messenger; perhaps later you will become my personal secretary and a freedman, whether you were once a pirate or not. Only see that you learn your lessons well."

He turned to the railing and pointed out over the city. "Do you see the customhouse down there on the other side of the market square?" He picked up the note from the writing table. "Take this to the chief customs officer."

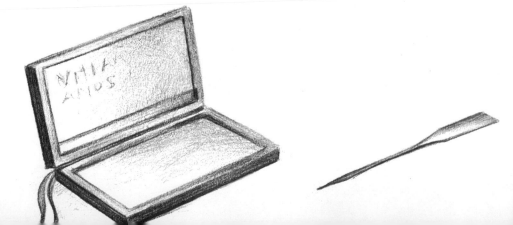

Valerian took the folded note and turned to leave the terrace.

"Oh, yes," his master added. "One other thing. Stop at the booth of Sidonius in the fish market. You'll find him not far from the customhouse. He will have a special fish for me—salted sheatfish imported from the Sea of Galilee. That's all."

Valerian grinned as he swung down the path. For the first time in over three years he was unshackled and free to walk in the sunlight, to go where he chose,

28

to stop here and there, to look around when he wished without feeling the lash. But his grin faded and his dark eyes narrowed.

"Watch yourself," he muttered. "Trust no man. They let your father die and trapped you into slavery. You are still alone against the world, just as before."

He pushed his way along the narrow, bustling streets to the customhouse. The seal of Maxentius got him through the guard without a word, and he delivered his master's message.

Then he found the booth of Sidonius in the fish market corner of the crowded square. The smell of rotting fish hung in the warm air. An old man with a long scraggly beard was bending over a gunny sack of fish at the back of the booth.

"You, fishmonger," said Valerian. "My master, Maxentius, sends me for a package of fish."

Sidonius nodded. He pulled a salted sheatfish out of a barrel and slapped it down on the board. "Shipped all the way from the Sea of Galilee," he said. "Eat it and you'll never die."

Valerian gave a short laugh. "The rotten fish of a galley slave is better than that," he said. "At least there's taste and smell to it!"

"As you should know, young man," answered the fishmonger. He began wrapping the sheatfish in a rag. His eyes twinkled under his bristling white eyebrows.

"Where I grew up, we threw away better fish than that," Valerian replied. "Even the cats wouldn't eat them!"

"And where is that, where you grew up?"

"The Island of Amorgos," answered Valerian, "far out in the Aegean. The home of men who fight to be free, who won't be ruled by gods or Romans!"

The fishmonger gazed at him. "Lad," he said, "what if I were to tell you how you *could* be free?"

Valerian looked at him sharply. For just an instant he saw something very familiar about the fishmonger's crooked brown teeth and his scarred hooknose.

"I'm a slave of Maxentius," said Valerian. "I
don't need anybody's help to find my freedom. And
what do you know of freedom—a flea-bitten fishmonger? Give me that Galilean fish!"

Sidonius handed it to him with a shrug. "You
sound like your father. But he used to speak better
of me, Valerian of Amorgos."

"What?" Valerian gasped. He stared at the fishmonger.

31

Sidonius' eyes twinkled. "I was not always an old man selling fish in Corinth. Remember back to when you were a little boy." Suddenly he looked out into the market square. "But now, begone!" he whispered. "A soldier is watching."

Valerian backed away as he was told. But as he made his way along the noisy streets, his thoughts raced through a jumble of flashing memories, trying to place the fishmonger. He remembered wandering along the cliffs of Amorgos Island, swimming in the clear waters of the cove. In his mind's eye he could see the masts and slanting sails of the ships that made up the swift and deadly pirate fleet. He searched through the faces of his father's comrades, the captains and rough sailors of the wild Aegean islands. But he could not place the face of Sidonius, with the crooked brown teeth, the scarred hooknose.

Finally Valerian shook his head. "A fishmonger," he muttered. "And what's this fuss about the fish of Galilee?"

As the personal messenger of his master, Valerian had a small cell at the end of the house. He lay on his cot, but he could not sleep. The words of Sidonius ran through his mind over and over again. The old, bearded face seemed to float before him. At last he rolled off his cot and pushed through the door flap onto the moonlit terrace. Through the open door of his master's room he saw the admiral bent over a

table writing in the unsteady light of a small oil lamp. Valerian saw the reddish light and the black shadows on his master's face. The oil lamp!

"That's it!" whispered Valerian. "The oil lamp!" Suddenly it all came back to him. The oil lamp in their stone hut! Sidonius! he thought. That's not his name! He's *Thalon!*

That was the man! Once he was the chief pirate of them all. It was many years ago, when Valerian's father was only the captain of a single ship. Thalon! The master pirate!

Valerian remembered the times that Thalon had anchored in their cove and climbed the rocks to their stone hut on the low bluff. He would sit late into the night over a small oil lamp, talking with Valerian's father. The unsteady light of the lamp's flame would cast shadows on his scarred face. His crooked teeth would sparkle. His eyes would laugh under bristling black brows. He had no beard then.

One day the news spread through the islands that a mighty fleet of Roman galleys had come to the Aegean to wipe out the pirates. But in spite of that Thalon called his captains together to plan a mass

attack on a large fleet of treasure ships passing through the Andros Straits. When the pirate ships entered the straits, the galleys of Maxentius swarmed out of hidden bays and scattered them to the four winds. Thalon's ship fled before the galleys into the teeth of a gale off the southern capes of Greece— "The Shark's Jaws," as the capes were called. The master pirate was never seen again in the Aegean Islands.

Then Valerian's father became the pirate king of Aegea, with his own fleets. Even the name of Thalon was forgotten. For pirates do not live long, and when they are gone the Aegean washes their memory away.

Thalon! Valerian thought. That's who you are!

Valerian did not have many days to wait before he was sent to the market square again.

"Oh, by the way, Valerian," said the admiral, at

his writing table on the terrace, "stop at the fish booth of Sidonius for another of those salted sheatfish from Galilee."

When Valerian got to the square he looked at old Sidonius carefully. He knew at once that he had been right. He was none other than Thalon, the master pirate, grown old—once the greatest fighter on the Aegean Sea!

"Well, my son?" asked the fishmonger. His lined face creased into a smile as he looked deeply into Valerian's eyes.

"Yes," murmured Valerian. For the first time since he had watched his father trapped and killed by the Romans he had found a man whom he might trust. He took a deep breath. "Another of those Galilean fish," he said.

The old man wrapped a salted fish in a rag and put it down on the board. "Have you thought over what I said?" he asked.

Valerian nodded. "I have thought of little else."

"It has been a long time since Andros Straits," smiled the old pirate. "And my hair has turned gray." His eyes took a distant look. "Many storms since then, and many calms. Many battles. Sometimes a victory."

Valerian searched the old man's face. He saw great sadness there, but also deep strength and a steady light. "My father loved you as he loved no other man, Thalon," he said. "He would tell me to trust you now, even as he would trust you himself, if he were still alive."

The old man's eyes glistened with tears. "Thank you, my son," he whispered. "Now you must go. But soon we shall meet and talk again." He handed Valerian the wrapped sheatfish from the Sea of Galilee.

"As soon as you say the word," answered Valerian. "Good-by—my father."

Valerian pushed through the noisy square, past the shouting merchants. For three years he had steeled himself to stand alone, without family or friends or trusted comrades. When a sick slave was thrown to the sharks, he refused to feel it. It was the only way he could keep his heart from being broken by their suffering.

But now his spirit leaped like a wild island horse suddenly unfettered. At last he had found a father! In the flashing moment of remembering Thalon, his loneliness had fallen away. He was free to be a human being once more, of flesh and blood, of love and anger, of feeling and of life.

You are risking everything, Valerian! he argued with himself again that night as he lay on his cot. You have dared to trust someone again! You are a fool! Remember how your soul died when you saw your comrades driven to the deck and branded with a white-hot iron, chained, and dragged away to the galleys. They had depended on you, Valerian, and you led them into slavery and torture and death. . . . For a long time Valerian looked out of the high window. Do you dare to trust any man, Valerian? Even old Thalon . . . ? He sighed. It was already done.

Suddenly Valerian heard a sound on the outside stairs. He rolled off the cot and quietly pulled aside the corner of the door flap. His heart leaped as he saw a figure step onto the terrace. In the moonlight he recognized the beard and the hooknose! But just as he was about to whisper, "Thalon!" he stopped short. For the old pirate had not paused as if he were a stranger to the house. He went across the terrace to the admiral's door and tapped softly.

Valerian's heart froze. His stomach knotted. His spirit turned again to dead, cold stone.

"No!" he gasped. "Not you, Thalon!" He sank back on his cot. "Betrayed!" he whispered. "Betrayed by my father's best friend!"

Then it dawned on him. The fish of Galilee! A password! he thought. So Thalon is a dirty spy for Maxentius! The master pirate has turned traitor to all his old Aegean comrades!

Valerian's eyes were cold and deadly once more, like the eyes of a tiger shark waiting for its prey. He reached into his cot and drew out a bronze dagger from its hiding place. Then he waited.

In a few moments the old fishmonger came out again, followed by the admiral. They crossed the terrace and disappeared down the stairs.

The moon cast enough light on the path for Valerian to follow them as they made their way down into the city.

"Wait, Valerian," he whispered to himself. "Let them get to the narrow streets. Find an alley. Then you can gaff the two fish of Galilee!"

The streets of Corinth were deserted and filled with black shadows. Valerian followed his enemies across the empty market square and into the Jewish quarter on the other side. It was a maze of twisting alleys. This was his chance!

But Valerian pressed back into the shadows as three men came out of the darkness and joined Maxentius and Thalon. As he watched, he saw them enter a house next to the old synagogue of the Jews. Valerian slipped past the entrance and down a narrow passageway. Behind the building he found a small back door. Very gently he tried the latch and the door opened. He slipped into the pitch-blackness very slowly, feeling his way, and finally came to some stone stairs. At the top of these he found a short hallway with a heavy curtain at the end. He could hear the low murmur of voices. A glimmer of light filtered under the curtain.

Valerian took a deep breath. Slowly, Valerian, he thought to himself. Don't slip now! One creak of the floor and all is lost.

At last he was standing behind the curtain. Carefully he pulled its edge aside and looked into the room.

It was a small chamber. The feeble light of an oil lamp cast shadows over the walls. He could see his master sitting at a table. Thalon and the other men were there too. They were silent. They did not move. Their heads were bowed. On the table were a broken loaf of bread and a large wine goblet.

Then Thalon raised his head and stood up. Valerian pressed back, his knife gripped in his hand ready to strike. But the old man made no move toward the curtain. Instead, he picked up the goblet with trembling hands, as if it held the very water of life!

"Beloved brethren," the old man said, "when the Lord had given the loaf, he took the cup. He gave thanks to the Father. Then he said: 'Take this, and divide it among yourselves. This cup is the new covenant in my blood.' "

Valerian stared around the edge of the curtain. Were they drinking blood? He saw the old pirate lift the goblet to his lips and drink, and then hand it carefully to Maxentius. Valerian could hardly keep from gasping as his master took the cup and drank from it and then bowed his head again. And so the cup went from hand to hand around the table.

Valerian dared not wait any longer. Whatever those men were doing, whatever strange magic they

were up to, he had seen enough. He had come for other business! Suddenly, he threw back the curtain and stepped inside with his dagger poised in front of him.

"Enough foolishness," he snarled.

The men looked up in surprise.

"Valerian!" said the old man.

"This is the end for you, Thalon! Showing the Romans where to find all your old comrades! Traitor to all the pirates of the Aegean!"

He lunged at the old fishmonger with his knife, but Thalon dodged and grabbed his arm as it came down. The men cried out and leaped to their feet. The table tipped over. The oil lamp crashed down. Flaming oil splashed on the wood floor and raced for the curtain. The room lit up brightly. Valerian knocked the old man down with a blow of his fist and then jumped through the curtain into the hallway. He dashed down the stairs, across the storage room, and out into the night.

He ran through the maze of black streets until he finally came out on the open road to the east port. He ran on and on, back toward the sea, toward his own country and freedom. . . .

A small fishing boat plodded slowly into the cove. It was weather-beaten. Its rigging was torn and shredded. In the still afternoon its single tattered sail hung nearly limp. The boat rocked silently.

Valerian peered at the low rock bluff rising out of the water. He could see the deserted stone hut where he had grown up. Along the beach a line of stone ruins was all that was left of their village. The savage ocean storms of three years had torn and beaten the roofs and shattered doors and window shutters. His village was gone, like all the other villages of Amorgos Island. Not a soul was left to welcome him home.

The fishing boat nosed through the small waves and ran aground in the shallow surf.

"Courage, Valerian," he said to himself. "It is no worse than it was. You are still alone against the world, just as before. All alone, Valerian. Even the gods are dead."

He fell down on the wet sand and wept.

The bright, early morning sunlight shone through the broken wall into the stone hut on the bluff. At last Valerian opened his eyes. The forlorn call of a distant sea gull drifted in over the water. It seemed to come from a long way off, as if the nearest thing alive was very far away.

"If I could only die," he whispered. "Even slavery was better than this. At least I was not alone!"

Then he began to hear a faint, pulsing beat. It seemed to come from out across the sea. He scrambled to his knees. Far out beyond the kelp beds he saw a narrow Roman galley racing in toward the island from the south. The banks of oars flashed and dipped steadily, to the endless beat of the stroke drum. The galley cruised onward over the water and finally disappeared past the point. The chill of loneliness seeped back into Valerian's spirit, and he turned away with a heavy heart.

"You're alone again, Valerian," he whispered, "just as before."

Later Valerian came back up from the spring behind the stone hut. He was startled to see the galley anchored in the cove, close to the beach. He slipped into the hut and looked down from the corner of the window.

"Valerian," said an old voice behind him.

Valerian whirled, reaching for his bronze dagger, and stared at Thalon, who was standing just inside the door. "You!" he gasped. "I'll kill you! Traitor! Traitor!"

"Remember, my son," said the old pirate, "I've killed many who dared to draw a knife against me. But listen to me, Valerian. That time you came to the fish booth you said your father once loved me as he loved no other man—that if he were still alive, he would trust me."

"No," whispered Valerian. "You're a traitor! He'd kill you on the spot for serving Maxentius!"

"I have only served Maxentius the Christian, my son. I have never been a traitor to old friends. Until the night you broke in on us, he knew me as Sidonius, the fishmonger, a brother in Christ—nothing else."

"You lie." Valerian's voice shook.

"It is the truth," the old man replied. "You know about Andros Straits, and how the galleys chased Thalon's ship onto the Shark's Jaws. Thalon died in that storm. He is no more."

"You're not dead," answered Valerian. His knuckles went white as he gripped his knife.

"A man was dragged out of the surf by some Christians who lived on the capes," the old man went on. "They nursed him back to health. It took many months. They taught him to know the Lord Jesus Christ, and when he was well he became Sidonius, a Christian."

"You talk in riddles," answered Valerian, frowning.

The old man smiled. "A Christian is one who believes in Jesus Christ, the Galilean. He was crucified near Jerusalem by the Romans and the Jews, back in the days of the Emperor Tiberius. He was dead and buried, but on the third day *he rose from the dead!* He's God's Son, Valerian. He destroyed death! And he can save you from death too, beloved, and give you eternal life. I know, because he has done that for me."

"You're crazy," Valerian spoke scornfully.

"It is the truth, my son. Believe me, I am telling you what I *know!* Trust my word, Valerian. Are you so wounded and full of hate that you don't remember how it was when you trusted your father? It was good to feel you could simply believe in him and know he would stand by you because you were his son and he loved you. That's just the way it is when you know the Lord Jesus Christ."

Valerian backed away. "I don't believe you," he muttered. "The gods are dead. You're lying to me. It's a trick!"

"Then kill me now, my son," answered the old man. He knelt on the dirt floor and bowed his head. "Drive your knife into my heart, Valerian, or trust my words and find life again."

Valerian stared in surprise.

"O Lord," Thalon prayed, "look down upon Valerian and forgive him. Open his eyes and break through the loneliness of his heart, and make him know the love you have for him. If I must die to show him, O Lord, I rejoice in your will. . . ."

Valerian gripped his knife and stepped toward the old man. He watched closely, for Thalon knew every trick. He saw that the old pirate's eyes were closed. His hands were clasped together as he prayed. Valerian raised his knife slowly in the air over Thalon's neck. He took a deep breath and—he could not bring his hand to plunge the dagger into the old man's defenseless back! Hot tears burned in his eyes and he stumbled away to the window.

"Get up," he whispered hoarsely. "Get out!"

The old man opened his eyes and blinked. "If you won't kill me, Valerian, then come back to Corinth with me, to learn of Jesus Christ."

"No!" cried Valerian. "The gods are dead! It's too late! Too late!"

The old man rose to his feet. "It is only too late if you choose to have it so," he said gently. "It's very hard for me to leave you here, my son. But as the Heavenly Father wills, so I must do. I must let you suffer through all this pain of loneliness until the hour comes that you turn homeward by your own choice."

"Get out!" cried Valerian, "get out!"

The old man turned and left the hut. To Valerian's surprise no soldiers rushed in to capture him. They really were leaving him there! Down on the beach he saw Thalon step into a waiting boat, which pushed off toward the galley.

The next morning Valerian left the stone hut and stumbled down to the beach. He had not slept through the night. The words of Thalon still echoed in his mind.

He stood on the beach for a long time, looking out across the water.

"The gods are dead! What a fool I'd be to sail back to Corinth and walk into a trap! But if only I could believe Thalon! If only I could trust his words!"

Even as he argued with himself he dragged the small fishing boat out and pushed it into knee-deep water. Without looking back at the ruins of the village, he climbed in. He hoisted the tattered sail and headed the boat toward the open sea.

"O God of Thalon," he whispered, as the breeze caught the sail, "I don't know who you are, but don't let this be another trick. Help me to find you and to be able to trust again and love again and never be alone. Help me, God of the Fish of Galilee!"

He took a deep breath and set the boat on course for Corinth.

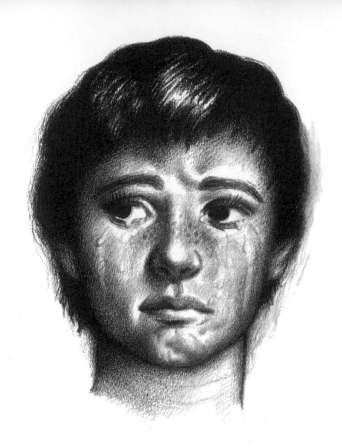

The Martyr Who Lived Again

LUCIAN RAN to the top of the cliff. He looked out over the deep-blue sea below, sparkling in the brilliant morning sunlight. Under his arm he held a package, and he carried a wooden shovel.

"O God," he prayed, "is this the day that you have made? I cannot be happy in it. Save us from the anger of our Roman masters, O Lord. Help us, by thy Holy Spirit, in the name of Jesus."

He threw the package down by a tree and quickly began to dig a hole. After a few minutes, he stopped to wipe the sweat off his face and push his black hair out of his eyes. He looked down the long slope toward his house. It was almost hidden behind a thick row of sycamores.

Then he saw Roman soldiers standing in a line in the yard. And as he watched, he saw his father and his brother Salonius being led out of the house by an officer in a plumed helmet. At the same time, he saw three soldiers running up the hill toward him.

Quickly he dug the hole deeper. His father had ordered him to bury the package of sacred books by this tree on the cliff, so they would not be found and burned as those in the church had been. They were the last Scriptures left for the Christians of Perga. He must not fail!

He threw the package into the hole and covered it with the dirt. The soldiers were almost up the hill. There was no time left. He hurled the shovel over the cliff, and then he turned and ran.

Soon he was over a rise on the cliff's rim and out of sight of the soldiers. He ran until he came to an old, overgrown path. It led to the crescent bay below. He turned down it and was hidden under the brow of the cliff. He heard the soldiers lumbering by above him with their sword chains clanging. Then he made

his way down to the rocky beach and hid in a cave
hollowed out by the sea.

He wept when he thought of his father and his
younger brother Salonius. By now they were being
led off by the soldiers to Perga. He shivered when he
remembered what he had heard about other Christians
in Asia Minor. Those who did not deny the Lord
Jesus Christ were thrown into prison. Then if they
refused to worship Caesar at the imperial altar, they
were pulled apart by the rack and thumbscrew. They
were killed by wild beasts or by fire.

His mind turned to the prison. Plans began to whirl in his head. If only he could find his way into the dungeons, he might help Salonius and his father and their Christian brethren to escape. He racked his brains trying to think of a way. But he had never been inside the prison. He would never know where to find them, or how to lead them out! His heart sank, for it seemed utterly hopeless. But he swore he would try.

All through the day he stayed hidden in the cave. Then at dusk he crept up the cliff and set off for Perga, eight miles away.

When he got to the city it was night. He tried to find some Christians who had been in the prison. Only those who had burned incense before the statue of Caesar had been set free. Perhaps one of them would be able to tell him how to sneak into the prison without getting caught. But every door was slammed hastily in his face.

"Cowards," he growled. "All cowards! Traitors to Christ, our true Emperor of Heaven!"

Lucian slipped down an alley behind the prison. The night was very dark. He turned a corner and came face to face with a guard.

"You! Stop! Stop in the name of Caesar!"

Lucian ran back down the alley as fast as he could go. But the guard's shout had stirred up a hornets' nest! Soldiers darted out of another alley in front of him. There was no escape! He stepped aside into a

doorway. The soldiers stopped in the street almost in front of him. He pressed back into the shadows, ready to leap. The soldiers could not see where he had gone, and one walked slowly toward his narrow hiding place. When he was almost to the door, Lucian sprang into him and knocked him sprawling. He started off, but another soldier jumped on him as he ran. He fell hard on the rough stone of the street. He rolled and fought and kicked. The soldier grunted and smashed at his face with his fists. Suddenly Lucian felt a terrific blow on his jaw. Everything went ringing and spiraling down into a whirling blackness. . . .

Lucian began to wake up. His head ached and pounded terribly with the beat of his heart. It was strange to hear singing—was he in church? His own groans of pain sounded muffled and distant. Then he thought he heard a woman's voice. "Salonius," she was saying, "Lucian is beginning to wake up."

He opened his eyes and tried to see. At first it was all dark. He began to make out the gentle old face of Mother Meona. And then he saw Salonius, his brother —Salonius, his running mate. He remembered how they had won the relay races together at Perga last summer. It was odd to remember that now.

"Shh, my son, do not try to speak," said Mother Meona. "Your mouth is badly bruised."

As he lay there, it dawned upon Lucian that he must be in the prison. He stared up at Mother Meona's kindly old face. "My father?" he mumbled. Salonius turned away and sobbed. Mother Meona looked down at him with great gentleness. "All is well with your father—now," she said very softly.

"Is well?" he repeated. "Now? You mean they—"

" 'Do not fear those who kill the body,' " she said, " 'but cannot kill the soul.' "

A great chill swept over him. He sat up, trembling violently, and stared around him at the Christians huddled in the dark dungeon, a great crowd of them. He buried his face in his hands. Old Mother Meona knelt by his side. She put her arms around his shoulders and drew him close to her. She pushed her wrinkled fingers through his black hair.

" 'Who shall separate us from the love of Christ?' " she said calmly. " 'In all these things we are more than conquerors through him who loved us.' "

She let him go as he slumped back on the musty, rotting straw. He lay face down, not moving, overcome with grief.

The next day it began. All the elders of the Perga church had been killed. The flock of Christ huddled together. They shivered in the underground dungeon of Perga's fortress. They watched in numbed terror as a red-haired soldier came in. He was stripped to the waist. His chest and arms glistened with sweat. One after another he dragged the trembling Christians

out of the cells. He pushed them down the dank stone passageway to the torture chamber. Hour after hour the prison was filled with cries and screams, for many Christians refused to deny their Lord. They were slowly put to death.

The people of the church were filled with horror. They waited for their turn, praying and crying to God for mercy. Some shrank back into the farthest corners. Some tried to claw their way in behind the others, fighting to hide.

But others did not shrink back. They stood firmly in their places and waited. Silently they prayed for courage and faith. They felt very close to one another, for together they would die for Christ. Their knees trembled and their breathing came hard; but their hearts were fearless and their thinking was clear. They looked to Jesus in faith. When the soldier led them stumbling away, they spoke strange words of forgiveness and blessing. But the red-haired soldier did not understand. He snarled and spat at them.

Hour after hour, he came in and dragged off the victims, one at a time. All through the day Lucian and Salonius, the two brothers, sat together in the straw. They did not speak to each other very much. But Lucian could see fear lurking in his brother's eyes. He felt it within himself.

At last Salonius moaned: "I can't stand it, Lucian. I'm a coward! I'm afraid! You hear them? Hear them scream?"

He shuddered. Lucian grasped his arm. He wanted to say, "Be strong, Salonius, have faith." But no words came out of his mouth. They stuck in his throat.

"Let's give in to them, Lucian! Please! Let's say what they tell us to say. Is it such a sin? Do we have to die? Do we have to be tortured to death like Father? Is that what Jesus wants . . .?"

Finally it was late in the afternoon. The red-haired soldier had gotten very tired of his horrible task. He stumbled into their dungeon and stood over them. His face was white and his eyes were wide with the terrible things he had seen and done.

"You! Skinny!" He pointed at Salonius. "On your feet."

Salonius cringed back on the straw and cried out:

"No! Please! Lucian, tell me what to do! Lucian! *Lucian!*"

The red-haired soldier stared down at Salonius. "Stand up," he growled. He grabbed Salonius by the hair. "Think I've got all day?" He dragged the screaming boy out of the cell.

Lucian sat very still. Tears came to his eyes. He

knew his brother could not hold fast to Christ. He was too young. He was too afraid. Lucian bowed his head between his knees. What he himself would do in the coming moments, he did not know.

Then Mother Meona was kneeling beside him. "Lucian," she said quietly, "the Lord Jesus will forgive him. Don't be troubled. Someday this will all be over. Salonius will grow up to be a fine Christian man. Then he will be able to tell others about the saving presence and power of the living God."

Lucian looked up at the gentle old woman. He tried to blink the tears away. "What of me?" he whispered.

"Come," she answered. "Kneel here by my side." Then she began to pray. "O Lord," she said quietly, "we thank you for your Son. Help us to feel his presence with us, living in our hearts, standing beside us. . . . You know how afraid we are. Turn our thoughts from this bitter suffering. Help us to see past this dreadful day to your eternal glory. More than life itself, we want to stand with our loved ones and friends, rejoicing forever around thy throne. . . ."

Lucian listened. At first the words did not mean anything. But Mother Meona prayed quietly. Peace and comfort were in her heart and in her words. Lucian began to feel that Jesus was there beside them, standing silently with his frightened followers. He could almost hear him telling them to be quiet and unafraid. It was not easy, within sound of the screams from the torture chamber. He thought of his father, who had gone through torture and death with courage, as a true servant of Christ. And now, in a little while, Lucian would feel great pain too. It would last only a few moments. It would be very hard. But then, time would pass and it would be over. He would be at his father's side again. They would pray for Salonius, his little brother. . . .

" '. . . And if I deliver my body to be burned,' " Mother Meona was saying, " 'but have not love, I gain nothing. Love is patient and kind. . . .' "

The thought startled Lucian's mind. God might help him to hold fast his faith even in death. But how could he love those who were going to kill him? He thought of the red-haired soldier, half naked, glistening with sweat, dragging Salonius out of the cell. How could he forgive the red-haired executioner?

" '. . . Bears all things, believes all things, hopes all things, endures all things—' "

Mother Meona stopped, for the cell door had clanged open. The soldier was slowly dragging himself into their dungeon. He nearly fell over them before he saw them kneeling there in the straw. He looked very sick and very tired.

"How long?" he muttered. "Must all you Christians be—butchered like hogs?" He straightened and stared down at them almost drunkenly. Dull anger smoldered in his bloodshot eyes. "Your fault! You made me this—*murderer!*" He looked down at his hands strangely. "May your God curse you for what you have done! Come on, old woman, we'll see . . . how a woman . . . eats burning coals. . . . Come along, old mother. . . ." The soldier began to sob. His shoulders drooped. He stood weaving on his feet, about to fall.

Mother Meona rose quickly to her feet. She spoke sternly. "Lad," she demanded, "is waiting any easier? Is an old woman stronger than you? Come along, then!"

The soldier looked up. "Come along?" he repeated. "Can I torture an old woman?"

"Wait!" Lucian cried. He jumped up. "Let *me* go! Not Mother Meona!"

The old woman turned to him slowly. "Are you sure, my son?"

"I'm ready," Lucian replied. He looked at the soldier. To his surprise, he felt great pity for him. "May the Lord Jesus not count my death against you," he said, smiling. "See? I come with you all by myself."

Lucian did not look back at Mother Meona. He marched down the dark passageway as a soldier of Christ, ready to face the last, hard battle for his Lord. He did not feel like a terrified prisoner dragged to execution. In Christ he was a conqueror! He prayed for his little brother Salonius as he went through the door of the torture chamber with the red-haired executioner.

The story of Lucian did not end in the torture chamber, after all, but almost fifty years later. In

60

a small Italian village called Cosarnum on the River Padus, far, far away from Asia Minor, an old bishop was dying. The people of northern Italy had always called him Father Lucian. He had come to them when the persecutions were over. For three generations he had lived in the villages along the River Padus. He had formed many churches.

It was a warm, sunny afternoon in the spring of the year. The bell on the village church began to toll sadly. The people in the shops around the square came out to see what was the matter. They saw Salonius the Greek, Father Lucian's brother, hobbling out of the church. They gathered around him. "What has happened?" they asked. "Why is the bell ringing in the afternoon?"

Old Salonius looked up. Tears streamed down his wrinkled face. He pointed his thumb over his shoulder. "Father Lucian—he is dying," he said.

The village folk hurried into the church. In a moment the pastor came into the chancel and spoke to them.

"Beloved," he said, "the time has come at last. Father Lucian is very near death. Let us kneel here and pray for him. Let us commit our bishop to the loving hands of the Lord Jesus."

The people knelt together on the stone floor. Some wept. Others stared before them with great sorrow in their eyes. For nobody could think what would happen to their village without their beloved Father Lucian.

At last the pastor rose from prayer. He made his way alone through the narrow passage behind the chancel to the old bishop's room. There he found the aged Salonius kneeling by the foot of the cot.

"Peace, Salonius," the pastor said. "Is he still asleep?"

Salonius nodded his head. The pastor sat down on a stool and rested his elbows on his knees.

"Salonius," he said, "I have always wondered—

how did you get here, so far from your homeland?"

Salonius looked at the old bishop lying asleep on the cot. "It must have been God's grace," he said. "You see, I found him wandering through the streets. It was several nights after—after they released me from prison. He had lost his mind. He was crying over and over again: 'O Lord, forgive me. O Jesus Christ, wipe away my sin.' And my own faithlessness was tearing my heart. All I could do was to lead him by the hand. He did not even know I was there. All he saw was that terrible chamber of blood and death.

"We went far away to the north, to the high mountains of Galatia. There in the deep forest stillness, his mind slowly came back to him. We made a pact together. If the Lord would only forgive us our great sins, we would go wherever the Holy Spirit might lead us. We would tell everybody we should meet about the strong faith we had seen in the prison. He felt he must make up in his life for what the church lost in Perga's torture chamber, where he—"

Salonius stopped speaking, for old Father Lucian groaned a little. His eyes began to flicker open. He looked at the ceiling. He did not remember where he was.

"It's all right, Father Lucian," the pastor said. "The Lord's peace be upon you. Good night, Father Lucian."

The old bishop turned his head slightly. His tired eyes opened wider as he peered through the darkness of the small room. "Father Lucian?" he whispered.

"Lucian? No. My name is not Lucian. Lucian had black hair. Mine was red. . . ."

Salonius buried his face in the blanket at the foot of the cot. Again the bishop closed his eyes. After several minutes, he was asleep. His breathing began to slow down.

"What did he mean—red hair?" the pastor asked.

Salonius raised his head slowly. He looked for a long time on the old bishop's serene, sleeping face. "What did he mean? He was remembering a time long ago. For you see, he is not my brother, Lucian. This man was my brother's executioner, the one I found wandering out of his head in the street that night. My real brother was tortured to death, for he held fast to Jesus. But we knelt together and promised —this man and I—that Lucian would live on through us. We promised to serve the church of Christ on earth, just as Lucian would have done. And so all these years my brother lives on too. Soon I too will be with him in the everlasting Kingdom."

The lamp flickered low on the table by the wall. The room was very quiet. The old bishop had stopped breathing. The pastor stood up. He smoothed the blankets around the bishop's body, then knelt beside Salonius. He saw the peace of God reflected even yet on the bishop's lifeless face.

"To us, beloved," he whispered, "you will always be our Father Lucian. Good night, beloved. Good night—Father Lucian."

The Death of a God

A HUNGRY TROUT jumped at a snoozing water bug. Over at the side of the small mountain lake a wandering bee hummed lazily around some bright yellow wild flowers. Brother Boniface lay in the shade of the pines and gazed up through the branches at the clear blue sky while his three companions lay resting nearby.

High above them on a cliff that towered over the water, a hunting party of nine German tribesmen glared down from behind some great boulders.

"Kill them! Kill!" growled a tall, dirty young man. His eyes flashed. "They come to drive us away from our god Thunar! I'll tear out their hearts with this knife. Thunar will like that!"

His chieftain lay on his stomach at the edge of the cliff, squinting down with the eyes of a master hunter at the four men far below by the side of the lake. "No," he said gruffly. "Be quiet, Friedrich."

The young hunter turned away with a sneer and slumped down next to a rock. He pulled his knife out of its sheath and tested the blade's sharpness with his thumb. "Gorgon, my chief," he growled, "these strangers must be killed. Why do we have to just sit here? Are you afraid of them?"

The chieftain whirled around and smashed his hairy hand against Friedrich's head, sending him sprawling in the gravelly dust. "Afraid, am I? You clumsy ox!" He rose up like a huge black bear and kicked the young hunter in the side. "Did you see their clothes?" Gorgon demanded. "They are Christian monks. Their God is a weak human being who was crucified by men. He was not strong like our Thunar! But that Frankish dog, King Charles Martel, has promised to keep them safe. We dare not risk his wrath. Let them go their way. They'll get tired of their babbling soon enough, when nobody will listen to them.''

They watched from the cliff as the four monks arose and began to climb up the trail through the forest.

Three days later the German hunting party returned to their own village. They brought only six wild boars slung on carrying poles. They had not seen a single stag.

"It's those Christians!" Friedrich growled. "Our gods are angry with us for letting them come here and stay alive!"

That night the village people gathered around the fire and sat on the ground gnawing at the roasted boar meat. Then, to their surprise, two of the Christian strangers walked into the circle of the firelight. Gorgon rose to his feet. He went toward them with his hand on the hilt of his knife.

"Get out," he ordered. "You are evil men!"

One of the monks held up his hand. "Peace, my friends. We have come to bring you good news of Jesus Christ, the Savior of men."

The squatting villagers murmured among themselves.

"Go at once, or I'll kill you!" Gorgon cried. "We don't want you here!"

"I am Brother Boniface," the monk replied, "and my companion is Brother Allain. We only want to tell you about Jesus, the Son of the real God—"

A roar of anger swelled up. Gorgon stepped in front of Boniface with his knife out. Its blade glinted in the firelight. "Another word, Christian, and I'll kill you right now. Go away and leave us alone. Thunar will throw his lightning at you for speaking of any other god!"

"Beloved," replied Boniface, "I don't fear your Thunar, for he is not God. May the Lord Jesus Christ bless you. We shall go now. Come, Brother Allain."

Gorgon followed them, with the stabbing point of his knife close to Boniface's back, until they had left the clearing and started down the forest trail.

Then they disappeared into the black shadows.

Gorgon went back to the campfire. He waved his hand to the elders of the village and led them off up the mountain.

On the other side of the ridge they came to a meadow where a great oak tree grew. It was very tall and very old, and it was burned here and there where lightning had struck it. They called it the Sacred Oak of Thunar.

"My brothers," Gorgon said, "let us pray to the great god of thunder and lightning. He'll drive away these Christian monks and give us back our peace!"

They all fell to the ground near the shadow of the tree. They did not get close to the trunk, for they believed that anybody who touched the holy tree would die in agony. They threw dirt and grass over themselves and rolled on the ground in the moonlight. They screamed to frighten away the God of the Christian monks. Then they crawled on hands and knees into the shadow of the great oak tree, where they thought only Thunar could hear, and whispered their prayers.

In a little while they fell silent. Gorgon began the final prayer, as chief elder of the village: "Holy Thunar, God of Thunder and Lightning," he whispered hoarsely, "I have been given to your service since the day I was born. All my life my people have worshiped you at this holy tree where you live. I pledge myself again to be your servant. I will drive these Christian dogs out of your forests and mountains."

Gorgon looked up suddenly, for one of the elders tapped him on the elbow and pointed. Back there in the silver moonlight at the edge of the meadow they could see Brother Allain watching them.

Gorgon snorted. "O mighty Thunar," he shouted, "smash these bugs, these worms of Christ! They dare not come near your holy tree!"

Brother Allain stepped back into the shadows and they lost sight of him.

"Let's go and kill them!" cried one of the elders.

Gorgon frowned. "Not now. Remember the French king. But Thunar will strike them down with fire and thunder from the sky! Just wait!" He smiled, for he trusted his god. "This ancient Oak of Thunar has stood since the beginning of the world and so will it always stand. We don't need to be afraid of these weak and harmless Christian monks."

"Praise Thunar!" the elders shouted together. "Praise his thunder voice! Praise his lightning fire!"

Weeks passed. The simple German folk of the forest villages would not listen to a single word the Christian monks said.

"Hah! You see," said Gorgon to the elders one day, "their babbling talk gets them nowhere. Do they think we would dare to dishonor the spirits of our sacred trees? They'll learn!"

The elders of Gorgon's village smiled a little, with narrowed eyes. Friedrich, the young hunter, sneered in disgust. "Oh, if they would just strip the bark from a single standing tree! Then we'd show them! I would tear out their stomachs and nail them to the tree!"

Gorgon gazed into the fire. "Nobody has been punished like that," he answered, "in all the years I can remember."

"It's the ancient German law!" cried Friedrich. "Don't you care about the mighty code of our fathers?"

Gorgon looked at the young hunter. "You had better learn the wisdom of your fathers before you try to uphold their code, Friedrich. Be patient. These Christians will grow weary. Long before winter comes they will leave our mountains forever. But the great Thunar will remain. He will light the flame of the sun in the spring, just as he has always done since the beginning of the world."

The days went by. But in all the villages hidden in the mountains and meadows of the great forest, not a single man or woman dared to believe the strange stories which the monks tried to tell them about Jesus Christ. Instead, they ran to their sacred oaks. They feared the anger of the tree spirits if they listened to even a single word the Christians said.

Then one gloomy, cloudy day at the end of June, Gorgon and the village elders got ready for the Fire Festival of Midsummer Eve, which had been held every year, as far back as anybody could remember, in the meadow where the Oak of Thunar stood.

The children of the village gathered pine cones and twigs. The older boys built a great wheel of sticks and straw and tar at the top of the ridge. Later, when it got dark, seven boys would take torches and set fire to the great wheel. They would start it rolling down the mountainside in a mighty whirl of flashing fire and sprays of glowing sparks. The wheel of fire would frighten the evil spirits away and save their village from hail and storm.

The elders whittled special oak sticks which Gorgon would rub together to drain out the fire of their god like sap. For they believed that the fire of Thunar was in every tree that had ever been hit by lightning. And the fire that Gorgon would drain out of the sticks would help keep the sun burning.

Later in the afternoon the whole village came to the meadow. They were ready to begin the Fire Festival of Midsummer Eve. Gorgon bent over his

oak sticks and rubbed them together to start the fire.
But then, suddenly, the four Christian monks
walked into the middle of the gathering. Brother
Boniface carried a great ax. The village people

gasped. The monks marched past them and walked right up to the holy tree. Gorgon stood up and shouted fiercely, but before he could stop them Boniface swung the ax hard and struck the Sacred Oak of Thunar!

The people screamed. Gorgon staggered back in fear. He stared wildly up at the high branches of the fire-scarred oak.

"Stop, fool!" he cried. "Don't strike again!"

But Boniface went on chopping with his ax. The furious village elders tried to scare the monks away with terrible threats, but they were afraid to come close. They were sure that Thunar would throw his thunder and lightning through the black clouds at any moment and kill the Christians. But the dark sky was silent. The cries of the people became a great murmuring and weeping as Boniface went on swinging the ax.

Then there was a crashing roar! The people drew back and hid their faces. But it was not their god of thunder. It was the great oak tree crashing to the ground. Branches and snags flew through the air. The dust billowed up.

The people stared. They could not believe it. They began to shuffle around the fallen oak, amazed that the Christians had power to cut down the very tree where they believed their god Thunar lived. They wondered why he had not killed these Christian men.

In the confusion of people milling around, nobody saw Gorgon, their chieftain, slip away into the forest and begin to run in great fear. Alone he went far up into the wildest part of the mountains to a secret cave and hid there from the anger of his god Thunar.

In the following weeks the monks chopped and sawed at the Sacred Oak, which lay on the ground. And after a while some of the braver men of the village began to help them. With the wood, the monks built a church over the very place where the German villagers had worshiped their god of thunder for centuries. The people began to listen as the Christian monks told them stories about Jesus, the carpenter of Nazareth, and about his love for all people everywhere. And they began to believe in Jesus.

One day Brother Allain walked far up into the mountains where he could be alone to pray. There, by accident, he found Gorgon in his cave. But Gorgon hated and feared the Christians. He tried to frighten the monk away.

"Gorgon, you cannot frighten the living God," said Brother Allain, stepping farther into the cave. "And you don't have to be afraid of him."

"I am not afraid!" cried Gorgon angrily. But his hands trembled as he bent to pick up a heavy oak club at his feet.

Brother Allain stood quietly, watching Gorgon stumble toward him around the little fire on the cave floor.

"You may swing your club with all your might, Gorgon, but my Lord Jesus Christ is stronger than your arm."

Gorgon swung the club hard, and it smashed down on Brother Allain's head. The monk crumpled to the ground. But Gorgon feared the power of Christ, for he had seen the monks cut down the Oak of Thunar and nothing had happened to them. He began to shake with great fright for what he had done. His legs and arms tingled strangely and his head began to swim. He stood swaying back and forth. Cold sweat broke out on his face. And then he collapsed on the floor of the cave.

In a moment, Brother Allain staggered to his feet and looked about him. He was surprised to see Gorgon sprawled on the ground. He stumbled out of the cave, holding his hand against the bleeding wound on his head. A few steps away he found a brook and washed the blood off his face in its icy water. Then he turned and walked wearily back into the cave and sat down beside Gorgon, holding his aching head.

Slowly the German chieftain opened his eyes. He saw Brother Allain sitting there next to him. For a long time they did not say anything, but finally they both smiled a little.

"Now will you listen, Gorgon? I want to tell you about my Lord Jesus Christ."

Gorgon sighed heavily and sat up. "All right," he said, "I am ready to hear about the living God."

Later, Gorgon and Brother Allain made their way out of the cave and down the mountain. They walked together through the forest, toward Gorgon's village.

"Do you see?" asked Brother Allain. "There are no such things as tree spirits. There is only one God and he sent his only Son to tell us that we don't have to be afraid of anything in this world any more. Truly, Jesus is our Lord and Savior! When you are afraid, come to the church. Jesus is present there to give us of his courage and strength. We have only to believe in him and to ask of him in our need."

They came to the meadow, and Gorgon was amazed to see the new church where the great oak tree used to be. He walked alone to the door and looked in. Then he stepped inside timidly, for he had never seen a church before. He stood listening in the stillness, and he felt the quiet peace of God.

In a few moments he turned and looked out the door. Brother Allain stood silently in the sunlight of the meadow, waiting for him. And he looked past the monk into the forest, where his people lived.

"I'll go to them," he said to himself. "I will tell them about Jesus Christ and call them to come back to this church. Thunar is dead. He never lived, but Jesus did. We will worship Jesus, the Son of the living God!"

Weep No More for Me

Two weary travelers plodded into the small Spanish village of Nadas. One of them carried a juggler's bag over his shoulder. The other wore a much finer coat than the first and carried a troubadour's mandolin strapped to his back.

"Come along, Pedestro," said the troubadour, "I'm hungry and tired. We've walked twenty miles since this morning."

"Ah, no, my lord," muttered the jester, scratching his head, "you may have walked only twenty miles, but I have walked nearly thirty trying to keep up with you."

"Humph," said the troubadour. "Don't complain about your short legs! I have more to get stiff and sore than you."

As they got to the inn, the jester saw a crowd of peasants coming toward them up the narrow street.

"Matrello, my lord, look!"

The troubadour paused at the inn door and looked around up the street.

"Bah," he said. "You dance for them, Pedestro. I can't be bothered to sing to peasants!"

"Yes, my lord," Pedestro replied. He threw down his bag and tore off his worn coat. Underneath he

had on a bright yellow and red suit. His jester's belled cap was tied around his neck, and he pulled that on. He began to dance wildly in the powdery dust of the street. But the peasants did not stop to watch. They laughed and went on.

Pedestro stopped dancing. He looked after them in surprise, for peasants always stopped to watch him dance.

"Where are you going?" he called.

One of the peasants turned. "We're going to see God's juggler!" he answered.

"God's *who?*" Pedestro asked. He scratched his head and shrugged. I've got to see, he thought. He put on his coat again and threw his juggler's bag inside the inn door. Then he set out after the peasants, who were turning into the village square a block away.

When he caught up with them, they had joined a large crowd gathered in front of the church steps.

"I don't believe it," the jester gasped, as he saw why they had passed him by. There on the church steps was a friar—a wandering religious brother. The gray robe he wore was dingy and worn, and tied with a piece of rope around his waist. He was not an old man, but he looked tired and sick. Yet his sunken eyes were piercing and his voice was strong and clear.

A few moments later as Pedestro listened he felt a hard rap on his shoulder. It was the troubadour. He looked angry.

"Pedestro, you dancing pig," he snapped, "what in heaven's name are you doing? Waiting to buy some holy beads? Come along and get me dressed!"

But the jester did not answer. He was craning his neck to see the friar on the church steps.

"Bah!" Matrello snapped. He pulled the jester away by the elbow.

The castle of Baron Fernando rose like a huge rock pile on a bluff high above the village.

That night the baron held a great feast to celebrate

the knighting of his youngest son. The banquet hall was filled with a hundred noble guests, all laughing and talking. Many servants swarmed around the long oak tables. They carried trays of venison and roast turkey, duck and goose and pheasant, and a hundred different sauces and pastries.

At the head table, the bishop sat gobbling up all the food his puffy fingers could reach. Next to the bishop sat Baron Fernando, and down the table, the baron's knighted son. At the end of the table sat the noble Matrello. And Pedestro sat at his feet.

"I say, Matrello," called the bishop, waving a huge turkey drumstick until he caught Matrello's eye.

"Yes, my lord?" Matrello called.

"Sing us a song like a good fellow," commanded the bishop. He lounged back in his great chair.

"Later, my lord," Matrello laughed. "The guests are still eating. But I've brought along a special treat—a true, live dancing ape!"

"A dancing ape?" cried the guests at the head table. "Show us the dancing ape!"

All the guests in the dining hall turned when they heard that. Matrello pushed back his stool and stepped forward. "Yes, my lords and ladies, I've brought you a dancing ape that also juggles knives!"

The crowd cheered. Matrello turned. He pointed toward the end of the table where he had been sitting. Suddenly a shaggy head popped out from under the table! The ladies screamed. Then, with a leap, the beast sprang out. It was Pedestro! He had an ape mask over his head. He hopped and skipped and swung across the floor like a tumbling, dancing ape. The guests hooted in glee.

Then out of nowhere came four daggers, spinning and flashing in the air. And out of the spinning flashes of glinting metal, a knife shot straight across the banquet hall. It stuck into the base of a wall torch. Slowly the torch toppled from its holder. But Pedestro was there to catch it. He flung the torch into the air in the midst of the whirling knives around his head. The dinner guests cheered wildly.

Another knife flashed out across the room. Another torch slowly toppled from its wall holder into Pedestro's hand. Two torches and two knives! The people gasped and clapped their hands. The daggers and torches whirled in a shower of flashing sparks.

Then suddenly Pedestro caught the two knives. And as the torches came down from the last toss, he caught them on the points of the knives! He stood with both arms upraised and the torches balanced far above him. The people were so amazed that there was complete silence in the great hall. Then the baron cried out: "Bravo! Bravo!" The whole room burst into cheers.

But finally the guests had finished their last jams and custard puddings. And they had seen enough of Pedestro. He went back to his place on the floor by his master's stool. He handed Matrello the mandolin and leaned back. This was always the part he liked best when they visited the banquets of noblemen.

As Matrello began to sing the jester remembered his own childhood. He remembered his mother sitting in their cottage singing these same old songs. He remembered the warm love his family once had known. But one day his father did not come back from the forest. Soon his mother died. Brothers and sisters were taken by the neighbors. He ran away from their Normandy village and began to wander

with a band of minstrels. He had never gone home again, for his father's lord would surely put him to death for running away if he ever caught him.

Servants came in and built up the log fire in the great fireplace. The room was dark and warm and quiet. The bishop began to snore.

Matrello, the troubadour, sang the wistful songs of a broken heart. He sang of battles, and of men who had gone off to war never to return. Pedestro closed his eyes to hide his tears. He felt that someday he would die like that without the blessing of the church. Once a priest had banned him from receiving the holy sacraments. He had called him a son of Satan for singing the tavern songs that made fun of selfish priests and greedy monks. If the priest said he would go to hell, there was no hope, for only a priest had power to save a poor man's soul from hell with the holy sacraments of the church. Pedestro trembled with fear as he thought of the horrible fires burning forever.

Then a strange thing happened. The troubadour stopped singing in the middle of a song. Pedestro looked up and blinked his eyes. There in front of the fireplace a shadowed figure stood as if he had suddenly appeared out of nowhere. The dinner guests stirred and sat up. They began to whisper from table to table. "Who is he?" But Pedestro saw who it was. He leaned forward with sudden excitement.

"Beloved children," the shadowed figure said, "the sadness of your songs melts my heart. But if we are moved by songs about men who have died in war and sin, doesn't the Lord God weep far more? Shouldn't we weep for ourselves as much as for men who have already died? God has loved us all. He has sent us his only Son. But we don't return his love. We don't love one another. And Jesus Christ is not alive in our hearts. How the Heavenly Father grieves because we have let his Son die in our hearts! Beloved, does the Father weep for you?"

The bishop awoke at this strange voice from the fireplace. Now he stood up stiffly.

"Friar," he said, "this is not the time or place for preaching. Be silent and go away. Go and walk the roads, or preach to the peasants. Perhaps the pope lets you preach, and the nobles of Assisi listen to you. But I won't have you preaching in the banquet halls of Aragon!"

"But, my lord bishop," the friar replied, "sin and death reach into castles as well as peasants' huts. Our Lord Jesus came to save all sinners, rich and poor alike—"

The bishop looked at him very sternly. "Don't try to teach me the gospel, brother! I've been a bishop since I was eight years old! I'll save what sinners I please. Now go away!" He turned to Pedestro. "Here, jester! Show this man to the gate. He too is a fool!"

The friar bowed low. Without another word he slipped away from the fireplace. Wearily he followed Pedestro out of the banquet hall to the castle gate.

"I'm sorry," Pedestro said.

The friar smiled sadly. "Our life," he answered, "is not supposed to be easy. Good night, brother fool."

"Good night," Pedestro said.

He did not go back to the banquet hall. He could hear the dinner guests singing. The pipers were piping a gay dance. Pedestro walked down a long, cold corridor to the first parapet on the castle wall. The night outside was very quiet and cold. In the moonlight, he stood gazing down the cliff at the dark, sleeping village far below.

"Brother fool," he repeated to himself. "He is certainly different from any priest or monk I've ever met." He scratched his head and blinked. "I—I wonder if Christ came to save even jesters?" He looked up at the starry sky. "O Father in heaven, do you care about Pedestro, the fool, even if the church has condemned me? Do you weep for *me*, O Lord?"

The next day Pedestro and Matrello, the two wandering minstrels, left the castle. They walked down the cliff road to the village. They went past the church in the square and started east on the low road to the coast.

In the afternoon, many miles from Nadas, they came up over a barren bluff and saw the ocean spread out below them. They turned north toward the town of Estrada, which they hoped to reach before nightfall. There Baron Fernando had a summer palace on the high cliffs above the sea. He had told the trouba-

dour that he could stay there for a few days on the
way back to France.

A winter storm was coming on. The cold wind went
right through the fur coats they wore.

"Hurry, Pedestro," his master urged. "We must
get to Estrada before the storm catches us. You
know I can't sing if I have a sore throat!"

"But what about the robbers of Estrada's woods?"
Pedestro asked fearfully.

"Hush," Matrello said. He looked around. "There
are no robbers in these woods. That's just a story."
But they walked closer together and faster.

Around a short bend, they suddenly came upon two men sitting by the side of the road.

"Robbers!" whispered Matrello. He fumbled with his sword.

"Peace, peace," one of the strangers said. He stood up. "We are only humble, wandering brothers. You don't need your sword."

His companion did not stand up, but sat shivering in the cold. Pedestro came closer and stared at him.

The friar looked up at him. He smiled a little. "Is it you again, brother fool?"

The younger of the two men shook his head in despair. "Brother Francisco is ill," he said. "It's this cold weather. And he has been very tired for weeks now."

Pedestro pulled off his heavy coat. "Here," he said, "put this on him."

"Wait," Matrello ordered. "What are you doing, Pedestro?"

"But he is sick and cold, my lord."

"Bah!" Matrello gritted. "Let these beggars answer for their foolishness. It's just a trick to catch our sympathy. Take back your coat!"

Then Brother Francisco looked up at Matrello. "Noble sir," he said quietly, "beggars we are—for Christ. We wander the world to preach his holy word. If that is foolishness in your eyes, don't trouble yourselves about us."

"I—oh, the devil take you!" cried Matrello. "Keep the coat, then. And you, Pedestro, can walk to Es-

92

trada and freeze to the marrow of your bones for all I care!"

"Yes, my lord," Pedestro answered. He reached down and helped Brother Francisco to his feet.

"Leave him alone!" Matrello ordered furiously. "They can't go with us!"

"But, my lord—" Pedestro said.

"Be quiet, you peasant!" Matrello growled.

Pedestro scratched his head and blinked. Then he straightened and threw back his shoulders. "Does the Father weep for us, my lord? Have we forgotten to return God's love when strangers need our help?"

"Please, beloved," Brother Francisco said quietly, "don't trouble about us. If God is willing, Brother Bernardo and I can get to Estrada by ourselves."

Matrello looked away. He sniffed. "Oh, very well, then. This peasant juggler wants you to come with us, so come along."

The four of them started off once more for Estrada in the gathering dusk.

Pedestro smiled to himself. "O Father in heaven," he whispered in his soul, "maybe you're not weeping so much for me now."

That night they reached the summer castle of Baron Fernando. A few servants met them at the gate. They did not want to let the friars come in. But Matrello angrily put the servants in their place.

"When the baron lets me use his house," he shouted, "I'll bring whom I please! And I please to bring these

93

ragged brothers! They're of higher birth in Christ than you, you scurvy slaves! Now bring in wood and build the fires high! Get the chill off this ancient barn, and boil some broth!"

The servants scurried to obey his commands. Matrello turned and looked coldly at Pedestro. "You peasant pig of a dancing juggler," he snarled, "go help Brother Francisco up to bed."

Pedestro smiled happily. He and Brother Bernardo helped the older man up the long, stone stairs and put him in a great canopied bed. They covered him with down-filled quilts to get him warm.

In a few moments Brother Francisco smiled up at Pedestro. "The Lord bless you, faithful jester," he said. "You have been very kind to me, both last night and tonight."

Pedestro bowed humbly. Brother Francisco closed his eyes and went to sleep. After a while, Pedestro and Brother Bernardo went over and sat by the small chamber fire. They began to talk.

"Does—does God weep for me, Brother Bernardo?"

The friar reached out and put his hand on Pedestro's arm. "Tonight, my humble friend," he answered, "I think God is smiling for you."

Pedestro sighed and blew his nose loudly. "You know," he said, "a juggler's life is hard at times."

"I know too well," the friar replied.

"But I can't be anything else," Pedestro went on. "I will be always walking on. From village to town.

From castle to palace. From tavern to inn. From
barn loft to haystack in the fields at night. It has
always been my life—to dance and sing and help
people smile a little. I've stood in village squares
soaked to the skin and tired enough to die on the
spot. I've made people laugh when I wanted to cry."

"Yet you go on," Bernardo said.

Pedestro scratched his head and blinked. He
smiled a little. "I'm a fool, God help me." He sighed,
and looked into the fire on the grate. "A man will
give up a lot," he said, "just to sing to people and

see them smile. Perhaps it's sinful to be happy. Maybe we're sinners for trying to bring gladness and a song to lift men's hearts for a little while."

The friar gazed at the glowing coals as Pedestro talked on about the minstrel life. And when at last he stopped, Brother Bernardo looked at him.

"You know, beloved," he said quietly, "I too have stood in village squares, footsore and trembling with cold. Francisco and all the brothers of our order—we're like you. We are God's jugglers. He has sent us into the world to gladden the hearts of men with the joy of Christ's love."

Pedestro looked at him in surprise. "Oh, but you are different, sir!" he gasped.

"No," smiled Brother Bernardo, "we're just like you. Only the song is different. We sing the song of divine love and eternal life. We would call men to rejoice in Christ our Lord."

In the darkness of the room, Pedestro began to smile. "That is a new thing—jugglers for God!" But his smile faded as he said: "I've always been afraid of God and the church. Could a person really be a juggler for God? Could he make me that kind of juggler? I don't want to die a lost soul. Could I be a juggler for God and help people be glad forever?"

"Perhaps," the friar replied. "If the Lord wills it. But now it's very late, Pedestro. The fire is nearly out. It's time to go to bed."

Pedestro stood up stiffly and stretched. "I had forgotten the time. Good night, Brother Bernardo."

He took a candle from the mantel and lit its wick in the embers of the fire. At the door, he turned and whispered, "Good night, fellow wanderer." He slipped out of the room and went down the hall to find his bed.

Early the next morning the troubadour stormed into the small chamber where Pedestro lay sleeping.

"Fool!" Matrello cried. "Get up before I kick you out of bed!"

Pedestro opened his eyes and blinked painfully, for he had stayed awake nearly all night, thinking. The sunlight streamed into the room.

"My lord?" he asked.

"Get up, get up!" Matrello ordered. "Do you know what a goose you've been?"

"No, my lord," Pedestro replied.

"I've just been up to that friar's bedchamber! Sick, indeed! I can't find him anywhere! We've been taken in! To think, I treated them like friends, and all because of you!"

"Oh, no, my lord!" Pedestro said in disbelief.

"Well, then, go see for yourself. That Francisco is nowhere around."

Pedestro sat up and scratched his head. "But Brother Bernardo is—"

"He's gone too!" the troubadour snapped. "Next time you listen to me! No more stray dogs or strange monks!"

Just then Brother Bernardo burst into the room.

"Brethren," he cried, "Francisco is gone! I can't find him anywhere!"

"You see, my lord!" Pedestro cried with relief. He shivered in the cold.

"Well," Matrello grumbled. "Oh, all right then. Go along. You'd better find him. It's too cold for a sick man to be wandering around this early in the morning."

Pedestro and Brother Bernardo searched the castle from one end to the other. They questioned the servants. They could not find a trace of Brother Francisco anywhere.

Finally they stopped in the courtyard. They did not know where to look next.

"Wait," said Pedestro. He scratched his head and blinked. "There's one place we haven't looked."

They climbed the long, winding stairway far up into the tower to the guardroom at the top. As the jester had guessed, the ladder was propped up and the trap door to the roof was open.

They clambered up the ladder. There on the roof they found Brother Francisco. He was sitting in the sun, out of the wind.

"But you are sick, beloved," said Bernardo gently. "What are you doing out of bed?"

Brother Francisco gazed peacefully at his companion. "Sick?" he repeated. "Last night, yes. But this morning I am rested and well. We can start again today. But the sun is warm up here. I needed to pray for a while. This is just the place to meet

God. I sing praise to him for the beautiful water
of the sea! Look down there. Do you see the ocean
dance and sparkle? That's the way my heart feels
this morning! I want to sing, Brother Bernardo! A
song of thanksgiving to God for the warm sun and

the dancing ocean and the warmth he brought to my heart last night!" He smiled at Pedestro. "Thank you, my friend. May you always be blessed with such willingness to serve the Lord Jesus Christ in love."

Pedestro knelt down in the warm sunlight. "O Brother Francisco," he said, "could—could a fool like me trade my suit of red and yellow for a robe like yours, with a rope around my waist instead of bells on my cap?"

Brother Francisco looked out over the sea, watching the swooping gulls and the pelicans diving into the water far below. And then, at last, he said: "If the Lord is in your heart. Is that what you really want, jester? We only try to be humble brothers. We only live to sing of Jesus Christ and bring holy joy to people."

Pedestro searched the friar's face. "I—I would go with you. If only the Lord would fill my heart!"

Brother Francisco smiled at Pedestro. "Yes, beloved. I think the Lord will give you what you ask."

Pedestro buried his face in his hands and wept with joy. "O Father in heaven," he whispered in his soul, "I thank thee for Brother Bernardo and Brother Francisco. Forgive my sins and live in my heart. O Heavenly Father, weep no more for me!"

Brother Francisco put his hand on Pedestro's shoulder. "Now, brother fool-for-Christ," he said, "you must go and tell your master, Matrello. And then get your things, for we must soon be on our way."

Brother Henry and His Bible

A BROWN-ROBED POOR PRIEST strode with staff in hand into the English village that huddled below Cawley Castle. He was a tall young man with blond hair curling under his broad-brimmed hat. Across the wagon-filled market place, he saw some angry tenant farmers and laborers lined up at a tax collector's booth. A serf cursed bitterly and handed over his money for the head tax.

"Dirty robber," he snarled. "Take food out of my children's mouths, will you, to buy a single toe bell for the king's dancing slippers!"

"Move on, move on," growled the tax collector, "I don't have all afternoon. Next!" He glared down at his list.

The Poor Priest walked past the booth as he crossed the market place. The tax collector stared at him angrily, with close-set little pig eyes, just about to say, "Get back in line!" But when he noticed the priest's broad-brimmed hat and homespun robe, he sneered out of the corner of his mouth, "Heretic Lollard whiner!"

The Poor Priest bowed. A broad smile covered his clean-shaven face. "A Lollard preacher of God's law, I am. Brother Henry Poole is my name, sir."

"Hah!" snorted the tax collector. "Leave these stupid serfs alone, penny preacher! Your turn when I'm through!"

But the serfs and laborers left the line and began to gather around Brother Poole.

"Tell us about Jesus! Read the Bible to us! We want to hear the Bible!"

The Lollard preacher beamed. He pulled a small book out of his robe and held it up. "Later, later," he said. "In the church, perhaps. I must visit your parish pastor, William Mew, and see. If not, I'll come back to the market place."

He set off down the village road to the parish pastor's house. When he knocked on the door, the housekeeper peered out.

"What do you want?" she said. "We don't give anything to beggars!"

The preacher looked at her coolly. "I have not come to beg alms, my lady. I am a wandering preacher of God's law. Is Pastor Mew at home?"

"He's busy," she snapped.

"Be kind enough to tell him Brother Henry Poole of Oxford would like to see him."

"Humph," huffed the housekeeper. "Come in, then. You'll have to tell him yourself."

Without another word she turned and led him through the richly carpeted hallway and up the stairs to a large bedroom. A fat clergyman was slouched in a great armchair by the window. The late afternoon sunlight flooded in on him. He pulled his napkin out from under his chin and looked with beady eyes at the preacher.

"Well? What is it?"

"I'm Brother Henry Poole, from Oxford University," said the preacher. "Good afternoon, Brother William."

"Bah!" snapped the pastor. "Father Mew to you, upstart!"

"I'm an ordained priest as well as you, sir," answered the preacher. "But do forgive me. I meant no harm."

"Well, out with it. What is it you want of me?"

"I'm traveling through Kent preaching God's law out of his Book," said Brother Henry.

"Then you needn't stop in Cawley, sir," answered Father Mew.

"We only try to strengthen and help the good Christian pastor in his work, where we are welcome," said the preacher.

Fat Father Mew glowered at him. "Who are you? How dare you think I need the help of an ignoramus!"

"Sir," answered Brother Henry, "the preaching of God's law and the reading of his Word is not ignorance. If the light of God's Word is hard on a pastor—"

"You insolent babbler!" sneered Father Mew. "The bishop will hear of this! Get out!"

"But, beloved," said the preacher, "I only ask the use of your church for an hour."

"I'll do any preaching that has to be done here!" answered the pastor. His voice was beginning to tremble. "Four times a year I preach! That's my bishop's orders. The serfs pay me to forgive their

sins and say mass. They don't need your cursed
English Bible for that!" He stood up and shook a fat
finger at the preacher. "You're a disturber of the
peace, Lollard! Wycliffite! You'd stir up the people
against the sacred laws of the church! Get out,
heretic! Get out of Cawley! I'll report you to the
bishop!"

"I'm sorry to have troubled you," murmured the preacher. "May God bless you, Father Mew. Good afternoon."

"Get out!" bellowed the pastor. His fat red cheeks shook with rage.

Brother Henry, the Poor Priest, returned to the market place. He was just in time to see the Lord of Cawley Castle ride into the village and rein up at the tax booth.

"On your way, publican!" he called to the tax col-

lector. "You won't bleed my people dry all in one day! On with you!"

The serfs growled in agreement. Brother Henry watched as the tax collector scrambled to his feet with his moneybag and fled between the wagons and carts. The people began to shout names after him as he disappeared out of the market place.

"The preacher's back!" shouted a stocky little serf.

The people turned and saw him. "To the church!" they cried.

Brother Henry held up his hands. "It will be better here," he said. "The afternoon light is failing. The church would be too dark for reading."

The lord of the castle looked down from his horse. "Now, who are you?" he asked.

"He's from Oxford University, Sir John!" said the little serf.

"A scholar?" frowned Sir John. "Down here?"

"He's going to read the Bible to us, my lord!" answered the little serf.

The nobleman stopped frowning and began to smile. He climbed down from his horse. "Hold this beast, Willie," he said to the little serf. He came up to the preacher. "You mean you read the Bible? In our own language? You don't tell fables and fairy tales? What kind of priest are you?" The people chuckled. "It's good to have you in my village." Sir John was smiling. He reached out and shook the surprised preacher's hand. "If you have no better place to stay tonight, you'll be welcome in my house."

"Thank you, my lord," answered Brother Henry. "But now the afternoon is almost over. It's time to hear the Word of God."

He climbed up on a cart and sat down. The people crowded around. The preacher drew the little book out of his robe and held it up for them to see.

"This is only one small part of the whole Bible," he explained. "It took me a whole month to copy this when I was at Oxford with Master Wycliffe, the good doctor of the gospel. I'm sorry I don't have more of his Bible to read, but I'm a slow writer. This little book contains only the Gospels of Luke and John."

He turned the stiff parchment pages, looking for a place to begin.

"Ah, here," he said. "This is a parable—a little story—that Jesus once told a great crowd of people. They came to him from many towns around. This is the story he told them. 'A sower went out to sow his seed; and as he sowed, some fell along the path, and was trodden under foot, and the birds of the air ate it all up. And some fell on the rock; and as it grew up, it withered away, because it had no water. And some fell among thorns; and the thorns grew with it and choked it. And some fell into good soil and grew, and yielded a hundredfold.' And as Jesus said this, he called out, 'He who has ears to hear, let him hear.'"

The people stared at Brother Henry. A few were frightened, for they had never heard the Bible before in their own language.

"What does Jesus mean?" asked Little Willie. "I've got two ears. Hear *what?*"

"Yes," said the people, "tell us!"

The preacher smiled broadly. "That's just what the disciples asked! So Jesus told them, 'To you it has been given to know the secrets of the kingdom.' " The preacher looked at the people. "That's what Jesus said before he explained his parable. It's been given to you to know the secrets of his Kingdom. But, brethren, does the church tell you those secrets?

109

Jesus gave them to you!"

The people stared at him silently.

"Latin," murmured Little Willie. "We don't understand what the priests say."

"Aye," answered Brother Henry. "And if you knew Latin better than the pope himself, you would still never hear the secrets of the Kingdom! For they're in the Bible, not in the Mass books and decisions of the church councils! All you need is to hear the Bible in your own tongue and you'll know more than all the cardinals in Christendom! So now, listen to what Jesus says. For if you hear his words and believe, you will be saved. No priest will be able to tell you to go to purgatory then! Listen!"

The preacher smoothed the page down and began to read again.

" 'Now the parable is this,' Jesus said. 'The seed is the word of God. The ones along the path are those who have heard; then the devil comes and takes away the word from their hearts, that they may not believe and be saved. And the ones on the rock are those who hear the word and receive it with joy. But these have no root; they believe for a while and in time of temptation fall away. And as for what fell among the thorns, they are those who hear, but as they go on their way they are choked by the cares and riches and pleasures of life, and their fruit does not ripen. And as for that in the good soil, they are those who hear the word. They hold it fast in an honest and good heart, and bring forth fruit with patience.' "

The preacher looked down at the waiting people.

"Do you hear that?" he asked. "Those were Jesus' words! The very word of God, the seed of the gospel, which will grow in you if you have an honest and good heart. The secrets of the Kingdom are in this book! You have a right to hear it and read it and learn it."

"But Brother Henry," said the lord of the castle, "Father Mew says that we would soon make mistakes and not understand, and then we'd go to hell for heresy."

The preacher's eyes narrowed. "Does Father Mew know more about salvation than Jesus Christ?"

The people murmured.

"My lord," the preacher went on, "what cruelty is this, to rob a whole kingdom of bodily food because a few fools may be gluttons, and do harm to themselves and others! Cannot a proud, worldly priest misunderstand the gospel written in Latin, just as much as a simple Christian can misunderstand the gospel written in English?"

"You speak truly, sir," answered Sir John.

The preacher smiled. "These are the words of Christ. They are true, my lord."

Brother Henry turned back and began to read again, about putting a lamp on a stand and not under the bed, and about the Gerasene demoniac. The people stood listening intently as the sun went down behind the western hills and the sunset turned from yellow to red to rosy gray.

Finally he closed his book. "It is getting too

111

dark, my friends. I cannot read any more. The writing is not good enough."

"Aye," said Sir John, "enough for today. To your suppers, peasants."

"But read more tomorrow?" they called.

Brother Henry waved and laughed. "Someday, perhaps. I must be on my way toward Oxford at sunrise!"

"No!" cried the people. "We want to hear more!"

"Quiet!" said Sir John. "You heard the preacher." He turned to Brother Henry. "Come, sir. Our dinner is waiting."

That night Sir John held a festive meal at the castle. Then Brother Henry was given a bed in the old chamber of the castle knight, next to the lord's own quarters.

It was after midnight when Sir John came in with a candle. "Brother Henry," he said quietly.

The preacher woke up and suddenly rolled over.

"What? What?"

"It's all right," said Sir John. "Forgive me if I startled you. I was hoping you would be willing to come with me. I've just been told that one of the old serfs of the manor is dying. He is a faithful, loyal man. He's taken care of me since I was a baby. Will you come and read to him a little from your book?"

The preacher got out of bed and rubbed his eyes. Then he climbed into his clothes and pulled his sandals on. He took his book from the table and slipped it into his robe.

"I'm ready, my lord," he said.

They swung down the moonlit road into the village. The houses were dark and silent. When they arrived at the peasant cottage out on the far side of the village fields, they found Little Willie sitting on the doorstep.

"Is Papa David still alive?" asked Sir John.

"Aye, my lord," Little Willie murmured. "He was as long as I was there. Father Mew ordered me out."

Sir John and the preacher followed the little serf into the hut. Father Mew was sitting in a chair by the table, mumbling Latin prayers to himself out of his prayer book. He looked up in annoyance. "I said to stay out," he snapped.

"Not to me you didn't," growled Sir John.

Father Mew squinted at him. Then he saw Brother Henry. He sniffed in disgust.

"Sir John?" groaned the old man who was lying on a cot in the dark corner. "Is it you?"

"Yes, Papa David," Sir John answered, as he knelt down by the cot.

The old serf fumbled with trembling hands and took hold of Sir John's leather shirt. "I'm afraid, my son," he whispered. His eyes were wide and blind. "I'm afraid. It's so dark and cold." He began to cry.

"Gently, dear father," murmured Sir John. He did not know what to say. "Don't—don't be troubled. I've brought a man who will read the Bible to you. Don't be afraid."

Father Mew stood up. "But he can't read that!" he whispered. "You can't. I'll speak to the bishop!" He picked up his bottle of anointing oil and his prayer book. "Papa David will go to hell if he hears that heretic!"

Sir John looked up at the priest. "Go home now, Father Mew—if you're finished."

The fat clergyman frowned and waddled out the door. But once outside he did not depart. He stood in the dark, listening intently. He had never heard the English Bible, and for all his mouthing of Latin he did not understand the ancient language of the church very well. He was curious to hear how the Bible really sounded.

Sir John had turned back to the old man on the cot.

"Have no fear, Papa David," he said gently. "Another priest is here. Don't be afraid."

The old man tried to turn his head and see, but his eyes were blind. Brother Henry came forward with

115

the candle and knelt by Sir John's side next to the
cot. He made the sign of the cross with his finger on
Papa David's forehead.

"The peace of God be with you, beloved," he said
quietly. Then he opened his book.

"I'm afraid," whimpered the old man. "So dark,
so cold." He trembled violently as he clutched Sir
John's hand.

"Courage, Papa David," Sir John spoke softly. "Hear what Jesus says." He looked helplessly at the preacher. Tears streamed down his face.

Brother Henry smiled. "This is what our Lord Jesus says, Papa David. He says it to you."

"To me?" whispered the old man.

"Aye. He says it to you, right now. Listen to me. 'Let not your heart be troubled. Believe in God. Believe also in me. In my Father's house are many rooms; if it were not so, would I have told you that

I go to prepare a place for you,' Papa David?"

"For me?" whispered the dying old serf very softly.

"For you, beloved. 'I will come and take you to myself, that where I am you may be also. I will not leave you alone; I will come to you. Because I live, you will live also. Peace I leave with you; my peace I give to you; not as the world gives do I give to you. Let not your heart be troubled, neither let it be afraid.' "

The old man closed his blind eyes. His hands ceased to tremble. His grip on Sir John's hand relaxed. The agony of fear softened on his wrinkled face.

" 'I am the resurrection and the life; he who believes in me, though he die, yet shall he live. . . .' "

Not long after that Papa David began to breathe more freely. Once he opened his sightless eyes for a moment and smiled faintly. He patted Sir John's hand. "It's all right now," he whispered.

When the first streaks of dawn tinged the eastern sky, old Papa David died. His heart was at peace with God.

Two days later the villagers gathered in the churchyard. Another gravestone was laid among the graves under the great old oak tree there.

Then Sir John Oldcastle climbed onto his best horse and set off on the road to Oxford.

Father Mew watched him as he rode off. "Where is he going, Little Willie?" he snapped.

Little Willie's eyes twinkled. He looked sideways

at the pastor. "Don't you know, my lord? That's the road Brother Henry took yesterday!"

"Bah!" shouted Father Mew. His fat face got red. "Bah! Bah! A curse on them both!"

He turned away and stomped back into the ancient, vine-covered church. "Heretics!" he gritted to himself. "The bishop will hear of this! We'll cut the tongues out of these Lollards! The people have no right to listen to them. I'm the priest! I'll tell them what to do! And I'll make them pay dearly for the grace of God and his church! Oh, how I'll make them pay!"

119

The Secret Trap

HANS KLAUFFEN, the big carpenter of Eisenach, rubbed his horny thumb along the smooth oak of a new crossbow. He set it carefully on his workbench and turned to face the little man who sat beside the door.

"Neighbor Albert," he said, "you worry too much for Monday morning! Why are you so troubled? Brother Martin preached in many churches on his way to Worms, not just ours. Yes, and it was wonderful to hear the true gospel of Christ preached. But that was nearly three weeks ago, and you've been frowning and whining about it ever since!"

The little man wrung his hands and shivered, although it was a warm spring day. "But," he whined, "the pope will keep the sacraments from every town where Brother Martin has been to preach. Then what will we do? We will all go to hell!"

The carpenter shrugged. He turned back to his workbench and picked up the steel punch to stamp his mark on the stock of the crossbow.

"You're a fool, Albert," he replied. "The Bible doesn't say that God's power and grace have to be funneled through the pope to get to you and me! If the Lord Jesus Christ chooses, my soul can rise to heaven even if the pope forbids it. Let him try to cut us off. The pope can't chain the grace of God!"

Albert frowned and clacked his tongue. "Oh, you are blind, Hans," he moaned. "We must not say these things, even in private. How could the whole church be wrong for a thousand years?"

The carpenter carefully tapped his stamp into the stock of the crossbow. "Have a little trust in God's Word, Albert. Are you afraid the pope will have himself carried into our village and condemn us? Not today, anyway! And even if he did, I would follow Brother Martin and trust in God for my salvation! Come on, Albert—smile for once. It's spring!"

But Albert hunched his shoulders and hugged his bony knees. "How can you trust in Brother Martin's word?" he said nervously. "The angels may strike him down for his boldness! Tell me, Hans Klauffen, did Brother Martin preach again after he left our church? No!"

"Angels!" snorted the carpenter. He laughed deeply. "Devils may beset him but not angels, quaking Albert! And devils can't stop the power of Christ from coming to his people. That's one thing Brother Martin has taught us! Fear the Lord instead of the pope, Albert, and trust God for once in your life!"

The children in the road outside began to shout that a horseman was riding into the village.

"Oh," moaned Albert, shaking his head on his scrawny neck, "since the emperor and all our princes

have been meeting in Worms, this village is never at
peace any more. Why must they send messengers
back and forth so much? I tell you, Hans, Eisenach
is going to suffer because of Brother Martin!"

The big carpenter grinned and wiped his hands on
his apron. "But *you* have been suffering for Eisenach for three weeks! Poor Albert," he laughed, "come
along and see what this messenger has to tell that
will give you more pain."

Hans Klauffen ducked out of the door of his shop and strode to the village square. Albert hurried after him, muttering and shaking his head. The village children had gathered around the messenger's sweating horse. The villagers offered the messenger sausages and pieces of bread.

"Thank you," said the horseman. "Your prince, the Elector Frederick, will be pleased when I tell him of your kindness to his servant."

Hans Klauffen pushed through the crowd and came up to the messenger. Albert fussed along behind him.

"Tell us," said the carpenter, "what has happened to Brother Martin?"

The messenger shook his head. "It's all over. The emperor will make him an outlaw now. We're sure of that much."

Albert hunched up his shoulders. "Oh, I knew it," he groaned. "Now he'll be burned to a powder!"

"No," the messenger replied. "He has twenty-one days of safe conduct to get back to Wittenberg."

"And then—?" asked Hans.

"Then," smiled the messenger with narrowed eyes, "the emperor and the papists will have to catch him before they can burn him!"

The villagers were silent. Albert again shook his head. "Safe conduct!" he said and clacked his tongue. "Hus had that promise too. They never let him get started home again. They burned him at the stake right there in Constance. A Catholic emperor doesn't

have to keep his promise to a condemned heretic."
The villagers nodded their heads in hopeless sorrow.
"They'll never let Brother Martin out of Worms
now," Albert went on. "Any fool knows that."

The big carpenter snorted. "Any fool like you, you
faithless mourner! Do you think God will let his
prophet be killed by the Romanists? Don't forget,
our Frederick of Saxony is very strong! Even the
emperor won't dare to break his promise!"

The villagers lifted their heads and began to nod
their agreement.

"Brother Martin left Worms in his wagon three
days ago," said the messenger. "He should be here in
Eisenach in two more days. The elector bids you to
welcome him and send him on his way."

He swung up on his horse and wheeled around, then
raised his fist in the air and shouted, "Luther!" The
villagers raised their arms in the Saxon sign of victory. "Luther!" they shouted back. The messenger
rode off down the Gotha road.

The next day a peasant stableboy came into Hans
Klauffen's carpenter shop with a crossbow. He nearly
fell over Albert, who sat just inside the door.

"Here," said the stableboy wearily. "My lord asks
you to fix this. He said to be quick about it."

"Did he, now?" replied the big carpenter. He took
the crossbow and looked it over. It was not broken.
On the stock he found the crest of the Knight Sternberg, and under it his own mark stamped into the

wood. Slowly he looked up and peered at the stable-boy. He understood. "When does he want it back?"

"By tonight," the boy answered. "He said to give you this note about the wood to use."

Hans took the note and read the directions. The boy turned and left without another word.

"Are you hungry, Albert?" asked the carpenter, looking up carelessly.

The little man shook his head hopelessly. "But I suppose I must eat or die. Death will come soon enough to my graying head, without starving."

"Or to your shriveling stomach!" Hans replied. "Go along, then. I have a piece of bread here. I'll have to repair this crossbow and get it back to its owner before nightfall."

When Albert had left the shop, the big carpenter read the note again. "To Wartburg Castle. Tell no-body. You will not be back for a week." It was stamped with the ring of the Knight Sternberg, his liege lord. He went to the writing table in the corner of the shop. It was very hard for him to write, for he had never been to school. At last he finished printing the words: "Went to Gotha with crossbow. May stay with brother a week. It is spring. Say your prayers. H.K." He set the paper on his workbench for neighbor Albert to find and picked up the cross-bow. He looked out the door and saw that the road was deserted. The village square was empty except for a dog sleeping in the sun by the well. All the villagers were at their midday meals.

Hans Klauffen took his coat from the peg by the door. With the crossbow in his hand, he slipped out to the road. He took long steps but tried not to look hurried, in case any of his neighbors should see him go. He whistled a merry tune, as if he were off for an afternoon of rabbit-hunting in the green Thuringian hills.

When he had left the village and was a good distance down the twisting road through the woods, he stopped and picked up a daisy from the roadside. He looked back. Even the church tower was hidden behind the trees. The road was empty of travelers in either direction. Quickly he set off away from the road. He walked with long strides through the woods, heading south.

H'm-m, he thought to himself. I wonder what my lord Sternberg is hatching up this time? He took the note out of his shirt and read it over. "To Wartburg Castle. Tell nobody. You will not be back for a week." He frowned and stuffed the note into his shirt again. My lord is full of secrets, he thought, and smiled. He is a good master. I wonder what he is planning?

All during the afternoon, Hans Klauffen walked through the wooded hills. He went far out of his way to keep hidden from the peasants working the fields of the shallow valleys. Nobody was to know that he was going to the Wartburg. And everybody for miles around knew Hans Klauffen, the big carpenter of Eisenach. He dared not be seen.

It was getting late in the day when he finally reached the foot of the mountain. Far ahead, above him, he could see the towers of the Wartburg looming against the sky. The forest was thick and dark. Before long he could hardly see the path. The evening sky glimmered through the treetops.

Hans Klauffen tried not to be afraid. He was a big man with great power in his shoulders and arms and tough legs. But the creeping night noises of the forest always frightened him. Had not his mother taught him when he was a little boy that devils and witches, goblins and demons ran through the forests at night? Yet he dared not stop and he could not go back. The nearest forester's cabin was a mile behind him. His heart beat fast and he wanted to run, but the steep path was too rough. Even walking, he often tripped over roots and stones. The goblins are snatching at my boots! he thought.

Then he stopped. Sweat ran down his face. "Hans Klauffen," he said to himself, "are you afraid of demons? Didn't the Lord Jesus walk alone through the valley of the shadow of death for you? What are you afraid of?"

He smiled in the darkness and then began to walk again. I'm not afraid, he thought. I'm not alone. Didn't I hear Brother Martin say that? I'm not afraid! I'm not alone! The Lord is with me! Whom shall I fear? Our God a mighty fortress is! "And though this world, with devils filled, should threaten to undo us; we will not fear . . ." On he walked, up the steep forest path through the blackness. "Yea, though I walk through the valley of the shadow of death, I will fear no evil: for thou art with me; thy rod and thy staff they comfort me . . ."

In two hours, Hans Klauffen saw the massive walls of the ancient Wartburg Castle rising up out of the forest against the starry sky. With a great sigh, he strode up the last rise in the path and came to the castle gates. He lifted the iron knocker and pounded three times.

In a moment he heard the gatekeeper's footsteps in the courtyard within.

"Who knocks?" came the challenge.

"Hans Klauffen of Eisenach," he called back. "Liege servant of the noble Knight Sternberg!"

The gate swung open on screeching hinges and the gatekeeper held up a torch.

"Welcome, Hans Klauffen," he said. "I feared you would not get up the mountain in the dark."

The big carpenter laughed. "I was afraid too, friend Franz. But I was not alone. The Lord Jesus was with me! Not even Satan or the pope could have stopped me!"

Franz grinned and pushed the massive gate closed with a crash. "Spoken like a true Christian, good carpenter."

The gatekeeper turned and led him across the courtyard into the castle. The flickering torch cast fleeting shadows through the passageways.

"This place is as silent as a tomb," the carpenter muttered.

"Nearly," replied Franz. "Nobody much is staying here now. Just our lord Sternberg and the castle warden. And a handful of servants."

They came at last to the quarters of the Knight Sternberg. The gatekeeper pushed the door open.

"He is waiting for you," he said. "I'll go down and get you some dinner."

The big carpenter went into the low-beamed chamber and knelt before his liege lord, who was sitting in front of a bright, crackling fire.

"My lord," said the carpenter. He held out the crossbow and the knight took it from his hands.

"Good evening, faithful Hans," he answered. "You have done well to come so soon. It's a hard walk over hills. You can eat here by the fire." He leaned forward and took the carpenter by the elbow. "Please get up, loyal friend. There's no need of formality now."

The gatekeeper came in with a tray of food and set it by the fireplace.

"That's all for tonight, Franz," said the knight. "Make up a bed for Hans in your quarters. He'll be down in a few moments. Good night."

When the gatekeeper had gone, the knight turned to Hans.

"Now," he said, "I'm going to tell you why I sent for you. But first I must warn you not to speak of it later to anybody. It's a secret which even the Elector Frederick refuses to be told. Nobody in the castle—not even Franz—must have any idea what we are up to, or all will be lost. Nobody in Thuringia or all Germany or in the whole world must know. If even a hint gets out, there's no telling what might happen." He smiled at the carpenter's frowning, piercing eyes.

"Now, the reason I sent for you, Hans Klauffen, is this. In a few days, you and four other faithful men will take horses from the castle stable. You will ride down to the edge of the forest below Eisenach and wait. And then . . ."

Several days later a two-wheeled cart came lurching down a rarely used back road, which wound and wandered east from the village of Eisenach through the Thuringian forest to Gotha.

Behind the driver sat Brother Martin and two companions in the straw.

Suddenly one of the men stared down the road. "Brother Martin," he gasped, "look!"

Five horsemen had charged out of the forest in front of them. The other companion scrambled to his knees.

"A trap!" he whispered. He jumped to his feet and leaped off the cart. Without looking back, he dashed into the forest undergrowth and disappeared like a surprised stag.

The horsemen reined up around the cart with their crossbows drawn and aimed at the travelers.

"You, peasant!" ordered the big man who was the leader. "Are you driving the heretic Martin Luther?"

"Mercy! Mercy!" cried the terrified driver. "That's Luther!"

The horsemen shouted and cursed. They knocked Luther's companion back into the straw and pulled Brother Martin roughly out of the cart.

"Run, dog!" they shouted. A horseman dragged the preacher, stumbling and running, down the narrow road a hundred yards until they went around a curve and were hidden behind the forest trees and brush. Then the lead horseman wheeled his horse around and pranced to a halt.

"Welcome, Brother Martin," he laughed, "in the name of our good elector, Frederick. We're friends, not papists, and you have run far enough!" He reached down a broad hand. "Take hold, and I'll pull you up."

Brother Martin quickly took the horseman's hand and struggled to get on the horse's rump behind the saddle.

"Thank you," he panted. "I haven't run so hard since I was a boy, God help me!"

The horseman laughed deeply and pointed a horny thumb over his shoulder. "Your friends back there will feel very bad, I'm afraid, thinking the papists have dragged you off to murder you. But it's better this way." He spurred his horse forward and the band charged off along the road.

Before long they took a path into the forest to keep hidden from the peasants in the fields. They wound through the woods, up and down the hills.

"I don't see how you keep from getting lost," said Brother Martin finally.

The horseman chuckled. "I've wandered these woods all my life," he said. "And only four days ago I walked over these same paths, from Eisenach to Wartburg Castle."

When they arrived at the foot of the mountain below the Wartburg, it was nearly dark. The horseman dismounted. "The saddle is yours, Brother Martin," he said. "From here on, I'll walk."

Three hours later, the exhausted band reached the top of the mountain and went through the gates into the courtyard of Wartburg Castle.

Brother Martin looked up wearily at the ancient walls of the castle. The blackness of the night hid his tears. "Is this my refuge or my tomb?" he muttered. "I would rather die at the hands of pope and emperor than hide in this silent grave like a common thief. God help me!"

Two days later, Hans Klauffen walked into the village of Eisenach. He carried his coat over his arm and the crossbow in his broad hand. He was whistling a merry tune, as if he were just coming home from an afternoon of rabbit-hunting in the green Thuringian hills.

He had hardly gotten into his shop and hung up his coat on its peg by the door when Albert hurried in.

"Oh-h," he moaned, "have you heard the news, Hans Klauffen?"

The big carpenter looked around at the little man. His face was the picture of innocence. "News?" he asked. "Don't tell me the pope came to Eisenach, after all!"

Frail Albert looked frightened. "Hush," he whispered nervously. "Haven't you heard? Oh, I knew it would happen. It's the first sign! Mark my words, our village will suffer for listening to Brother Martin!"

"Sign?" asked the big carpenter. "What sign? What are you talking about? Stop shivering and make sense, quaking Albert."

"If you hadn't gone off to visit your brother in Gotha, you would have been here when it happened," replied Albert. He clacked his tongue. "They have killed Brother Martin! A whole troop of imperial officers caught him not five miles from here. They say there must have been a hundred Catholic nobles in the party. And they practically tore poor Luther apart. They shot their crossbows at the driver, but he stood up on the cart and told them that Brother Martin wasn't Luther at all. Oh, how he tried to talk them out of taking poor Brother Martin! But at last the soldiers pulled them all off the cart. They threw a rope around Luther's neck and dragged him away. Now it's all over. They've murdered him!"

Albert slumped to the stool beside the door. The big carpenter stood looking down at him. "Luther is not dead," he said quietly.

"He is, he is," moaned the little man. "Murdered. Hanged. Torn to pieces!" He wrung his hands and shivered, although it was a warm spring day.

"Somehow I can't believe it," said the big carpenter. He tried not to smile. "I'll never believe it. They can't kill Brother Martin. Luther will live on, God help him."

He looked down at the crossbow in his hand, then propped it against the wall beside his coat.

"A hundred nobles, did you say?"

Frail Albert nodded his head sorrowfully on his scrawny neck and stared at his bony knees. "Maybe even a hundred and fifty."

The big carpenter smiled to himself. He shrugged his broad shoulders and set about his day's work.

The Mist at Noon

IT'S JOHN KNOX COMING!" cried Malcolm Macrae.
He ran out of his cobbler's shop and began to skirl
a call to arms on his bagpipe.

In on the seacoast road came John Knox, riding
a powerful black horse fit for a king in battle. The
people of Crail were ready for him. They ran beside
him and swarmed into the square as he reined up at
the well. They cheered him as he climbed down from

his horse. He was a short man, too small to be a hero, except for his broad shoulders. His black hair and black beard flew in the wind. His deep-set eyes flashed and sparkled.

"Where is your kirk?" he called.

"To the kirk, the kirk!" shouted the people.

The town peace officer, in his constable's purple coat and plumed hat, pushed through the crowd.

"I'm Rory Harris, sir," he shouted over the noise. "Welcome to Crail! We've been waiting for you since noon! The kirk is ready, swept of cobwebs and trash! The rickety pulpit's been repaired. Come, Master Knox! Follow me!"

When they got to the small church down the cliff lane, Rory Harris took his stand on the steps.

"Now be still," he shouted. "Master Knox is going to preach for us. You'll hear him out! Not a man's to leave the kirk till he says the word! Now, enter in silence and hear the word of God as it should be —in the name of Christ and his true kirk!"

The people poured into the church. John Knox stood in the pulpit, waiting patiently, and searched their faces.

"Brethren," he began, "for four years I've waited and prayed for this hour. By the unsearchable will of God, I've been an exile, and now at last he's led me home. Five weeks ago today I landed, just in time to join the true preachers of the Reformed Kirk in Dundee. In time, I say, to be outlawed with them by our two-faced, popish queen regent and her French spies!"

The preacher's voice grew louder, his eyes began to flash, as he told his story.

"Five weeks ago she ordered the preachers of God's truth to come for trial at Stirling Castle. So we set out from Dundee, a small handful, armed only with His holy Word! And who stood with us then? Only an escort of country lairds from Fife and Angus. Not a single great noble among them! But now five weeks have passed, and who has come to stand with us? No less than the greatest man in Scotland—a king's son, James Stewart, the prior of St. Andrews! And who else? Five earls of the realm and the whole people of Scotland!"

His voice rang through the small church. The people began to sit on the edge of their seats, for they were stirred by the strong tone of his voice.

"The battle's called," he said quietly, but with great power. "The holy war's declared! Only the sovereign God can know whether Scotland will go free in the name of Christ and his true kirk, or back to slavery in the name of the French regent, Mary Guise!

"And why should Scotland be ruled by such a woman, a French princess? We are ground into the dust of our own soil by the heels of Satan's priestly mummers and their Latin Mass. They'd have us bow to cursed idols, which we ought to smash and burn!

Aye, and it's little enough, for the Catholics are burning our Protestant brethren at the stake in Spain right now! Let God's wrath do the rest! Let God's avenging anger burn them for stealing our lands and robbing our people, for trying to sell perdition for two pennies and the gates of heaven for a thousand silver crowns!"

The church shook with his thundering voice. It looked as if he would break the pulpit in pieces and fly out of it!

"In the name of Almighty God," he cried, "I call you to do battle for Christ! Cleanse the kirks and chapels of fools' idols and devils' altars! Turn out the drowsy monks and faithless priests!"

For an hour Master Knox preached on, until his anger soared and his words set fire to the hearts of the people.

And when he was through, the people rose up in a great roar. They tore the statues of the saints from their niches and ripped the pictures from the walls. They dragged the tarnished clergy robes out of cobwebbed closets. They gathered the books of Latin services out of dust-filled cupboards. They built a roaring fire outside the church in the gathering dusk and watched the leaping flames burn all the rubbish up. When at last the fire died, the church was bare.

Rory Harris, the town constable, walked along with the preacher back to the village.

"What will come of all this, Master Knox?" he asked. "The things we are doing will lead to trouble for sure. I hear the regent and her French troops are gathered not fifty miles from here."

"God will win, Rory. Scotland's ready to do battle for the Lord now. The past ten years have brought a great change. But the regent and her pope will not give up without a hard fight!"

Rory kicked the stones in the path as they walked along. "That's rebellion," he muttered. "Once we start, there's no turning back. Do you really think we're strong enough for that?"

The preacher smiled. "Aye," he said. "The everlasting God, the Lord, the Creator of the ends of the earth, fainteth not, neither is weary. They that wait upon the Lord shall renew their strength. They shall mount up with wings like eagles. They shall run, and not be weary. They shall walk, and not faint."

Rory grunted. "Your words are powerful," he said.

"They are not my words, constable!" the preacher replied. "'Tis the Word of God and his promise. The people of his kirk must learn to read it for themselves if they'd be strong and free and brave!"

The embers in the big stone fireplace glowed red. Rory Harris turned the pages of the heavy Bible in his lap and sighed.

"'Tis a powerful book, Margaret," he said to his wife. "The given word of God Almighty! It's worth fighting for, I do believe!"

"But not tonight, Rory," she smiled. "Do not get stirred up about it again. Come along to your rest. Must you read the night away again? Since Master Knox was here last week, you have done little else."

Rory pushed himself up from his leather chair and put the Bible on the table. "But the long night will

144

only pass away," he answered, "when true sons of God read this book and find the courage to be free!"

His wife turned to go up the stairs. "Don't wake the babies as you come," she said.

"All right, all right! I'm coming, woman!"

He took the brass snuffer from the mantel and put out the candles. At the window he paused and gazed into the peaceful night. Out there above the cold waters of the North Sea the moon soared in the crystal sky. A low bank of fog lay a mile offshore. Then wearily he made his way upstairs and went to bed.

Later in the night, Rory felt himself being shaken.

"Rory!" his wife was whispering. "Wake up, quick!"

He opened his eyes. The room was dark. And then he heard somebody calling.

"Constable! Constable Harris!"

He groaned as he rolled out of bed. He stumbled over to the window and called down: "Hold, there! What do you want?"

"Message from St. Andrews!" called a horseman.

"All right," Rory grumbled, "I'll come down." He turned and felt his way downstairs, muttering to him-

self about being awakened in the middle of the night. He opened the door and glowered at the messenger.

"Bring your men!" said the horseman. "The lords are calling us to St. Andrews! The queen regent and her French troops are moving up from Falkland, trying to catch us by surprise!"

Rory was suddenly wide awake. A cold chill passed over him as the messenger's words sank in.

"We're trapped!" whispered Rory. "How much time do we have?"

"None," said the messenger. "We need all the men of Fife by daybreak. Every spearman you've got! If not, the battle's lost for Knox and the true kirk!"

"On your way, then," Rory ordered. "We'll be there in three hours." He looked up at the sky. The fog had rolled in over the coast and blotted out the moon and stars.

"It's nearly midnight now," said the messenger. "There's no time to lose!" He swung up on his sweat-covered horse and spurred off down the road.

Rory turned back into the house and closed the door. He leaned wearily against it in the darkness. He was not afraid to fight, but the thought hammered at his mind: What have we done? Must we die for our faith? Is it really worth that much, after all?

He climbed the stairs and sat down on the edge of the bed.

"I heard," whispered his wife.

"There's no turning back now," answered Rory. "I've said we would fight for the word of God. I did mean that, didn't I, Margaret?"

In half an hour the men of Crail had gathered in the village square. The women came with them, and they stood shivering in the cold mist of the night.

"Let us pray," said Rory. "Almighty God, give us courage now to stand up for Christ our Lord. Forgive us our sins. If it be thy will, let us stay alive in the battle to come. But if we never see our families again in this life, hold them and us in thy mercy. Thine be the glory, through Jesus Christ our Lord. Amen."

The women wept as they bade good-by to their husbands and fathers. Then the men set off up the St. Andrews road, to the skirling whine of Malcolm Macrae's bagpipe.

For two hours they marched, and at last they entered the gates of St. Andrews. They joined hundreds of other villagers from the countryside of Fife and Angus. Rory Harris went to the courtyard of the castle. There the constables and town officers were waiting for their orders.

"What news?" he asked the burgess of Kingsbarns.

" 'Tis not good, Rory," answered the burgess, "not good at all. They say the regent has six thousand foot soldiers and a thousand horse three miles the other side of Cupar. And we've no more than two thousand spears so far. Two thousand, Rory! One of ours for every three of theirs!"

Rory frowned. "And the lords want us to fight? Three to one is no battle. It will be a massacre of us all!"

The burgess nodded his head sorrowfully. "But at least the Earl of Argyll has a hundred cavalry troops," he said. "Brave laddies they are! They rode out and took Cupar village at dusk, and not a moment too soon! The regent's outposts were already there, and they drove them out." The burgess shook his head. "How a hundred horse can hold it, I don't know. The regent's cavalry won't wait a minute past daybreak!"

There was a short command in the courtyard. Lord

James Stewart, the prior of St. Andrews, and Lord Lorne, the earl of Argyll, came out of the castle. The prior held up his hands.

"Welcome, loyal Scots," he said. "You have answered the call quickly. We only pray to God that more men will arrive before the night is over. Now, listen, here's what you must do, if God be willing. Our men still hold Cupar, ten miles to the west. The loyal men of the village have come back with me to lead you across the moors. It's faster that way. Take

your positions on the slopes of Cupar Moor, this side of the Eden stream. When more men arrive, we'll send them out to back you up. Fear not. Be brave! God save us!"

"Amen!" said the constables and town officers. Then they marched out of the courtyard, gathered their men, and started off across the lonely moors.

At daybreak, Rory Harris and his men were on the rough slopes of Cupar Moor. Their section of the line

was divided by a shrub-filled ravine. Around a short bend behind them, the ravine deepened into a small hollow with a pond and a grove of young beech trees. Rory placed his men astride the ravine in two lines, thirty in front and thirty behind. In the hollow he placed twenty men in reserve. Then they dug in to wait for the mist to lift.

"Rory," whispered the cobbler of Crail.

"Is it you, Malcolm?"

"Aye," whispered the cobbler. "This cursed fog!"

"Do not curse it," said Rory. "They'll not risk attacking till it lifts. The longer the mist lies low and thick, the better chance we'll have, for the more of our men will get here to back us up. Only God knows if they'll arrive before the battle starts."

Malcolm grunted and sniffed. "The heather's sweet in June," he said. " 'Twill make our funeral wreath. Three to one—the regent's got a bloody death for us!"

Rory stared glumly into the thick mist. "Aye, three to one," he answered. Suddenly his eyes narrowed. "But before the mist goes up we'll make it three to two!"

"How?" asked Malcolm. "Where are our troops? Maybe no more will come!"

Rory stood up and frowned. "They've got to! But look sharp now. I'm going back to the hollow there."

As the morning got brighter and turned the heavy gray fog to white, Rory put his twenty reserves to work. They cut down the straight young beeches that grew around the pond and trimmed their twigs away.

Then he tore his blue shirt into thin strips, like the pennants on their spears, and tied them to the poles.

"Now, brothers," he said, "go to the ravine and give each man a second spear! They'll be useless in a fight, but from the field the enemy won't know it! Then when the mist lifts, the regent's infantry will think they see two men of Crail for every one! Their hearts may weaken. Then we'll have our chance!"

Softly the men said: "Amen! Amen!" and set off.

Through the long hours of the morning the men of Crail sat hidden on the slopes of Cupar Moor. They waited for the mist to lift, wondering if any of them would live to see the night and their families again. Every half hour Rory sent a scout down the slope to the edge of the Eden stream. Now and then they reported the sound of moving enemy troops coming from the regent's camp.

At last, Rory said: "Do you see anything yet, Malcolm? My eyes are burning out, trying to look through this fog!"

The cobbler shook his head. "How long has it been?" he asked. "It seems as if we've been sitting here since the beginning of the world, all by ourselves. This mist can't hold much longer. Why doesn't a messenger come and tell us what support we have?"

Rory did not answer at first. But then, finally, he whispered, as if to himself: "I don't know. Sometimes I don't know why we're here at all, waiting to be slaughtered. It makes a man wonder if God is on our side, after all!"

"Hush, Rory," answered Malcolm. "We'll probably be killed this day, but if we die and the battle is lost, God will still reign! I only pray that we are on his side, not he on ours."

A feeling of anger began to rise in Rory's heart. "Cobbler," he answered roughly, "am I the only one whose faith is weak? I can die as bravely as you!"

The cobbler shrugged and grinned. "Do not stir my Highland blood, Rory Harris. We are to fight the enemy, not each other."

"Well—" grumbled Rory. "Aye, then. It is the fog making us jumpy. Come on—I can't stand this waiting any more. We'll go down to the stream and see the enemy for ourselves, if we can."

He waved at his men to stay where they were. Then he and Malcolm made their way down the slope toward the Eden stream. The mist blew thinner in the soft breeze. They looked back, and could just make out the massed spears, real and unreal, blocking the ravine and the approach to the moor. In the fog they looked like all the spears of the Fife coast.

"Let the regent's cavalry see that, anyway!" said Rory softly. "They'll have a real report to make!"

They skirted along the stream bank for a hundred yards.

"Far enough, Rory," whispered Malcolm. "We'll go too far. The fog might lift any time."

"Aye," Rory said. "But see here! A footbridge, as I expected. If we can stop them from using this, they'll have to ford the stream to get across to us.

Come on, get busy! We've got to tear this thing out!"

The two of them went to work fast with their knives and a small hatchet. The old bindings of the footbridge finally came apart and they waded out into the stream. They tore down the planks and let them float away. Then they got into deep water and had to swim under the bridge to work.

Suddenly they heard a distant command out in the field, from the enemy camp. They stopped and listened.

"Look!" gasped Malcolm. "The mist is beginning to lift!"

"Dive!" Rory whispered, pointing to the overgrown stream bank on the enemy side. "Get under there!"

They ducked under the water and began to swim with the current toward the brush that lined the stream. When they were in amongst the reeds and tall grass, they came up. Carefully they peered out across the field. The mist was lifting fast.

Stretched out before them, all the way to the hills beyond, they saw enemy spears, massed troops, line on line. A thousand French horsemen were mounting and coming around into position.

The regent's field officers were out in front, trying to hold their prancing horses. At the fore, on a great white charger, rode Lord d'Oysel, the regent's French general, wearing a broad, plumed hat.

"Come on," Rory gasped, "swim for it! We've got to get back to the slope!"

They pushed off from the bank and swam for their

own side of the stream as fast as they could go. At last they clambered out and ran up the slope toward their own line. But just as they reached the ravine, a great murmur went up. The men of Crail rose to their feet and stared and pointed.

Rory and Malcolm whirled around and saw a sight that made their hearts leap. For as the mist lifted higher and the whole Eden valley cleared, they saw their own army!—a great mass of militia poised and ready for battle! All the town bands were massed on the field in front of Cupar village. The banners of Dundee and St. Andrews, of Perth, Munross, and Lothian, were whipping in the breeze! Their bagpipes began to skirl a fierce battle song! And at their head were all the lords of the Reformed Church standing in their stirrups, with swords unsheathed.

Rory looked back at the enemy troops across the field. They stood waiting for the command to charge. But then the French general, Lord d'Oysel, wheeled around and cantered back to his field officers. He had not expected a pitched battle with equal forces.

The night before he had thought he faced only two thousand spears of Fife and Angus. But now he saw the army of Stewart and Argyll, as big as his own.

In a moment a horseman broke out from the enemy line with a white flag of truce and trotted to the center of the field. It was the sign! The fight was over before it started!

Rory and Malcolm and all the men of Crail stood on the slope and breathed a great sigh of relief, half laughing and half crying. All down the line, along the rising slope of Cupar Moor, the men of Fife and Angus felt as if they had been saved from certain slaughter by a miracle.

In a few moments the regent's forces withdrew from the field and broke up their battle formation. It was the signal for the army of Stewart and Argyll to leave their battle lines as well.

Rory quietly called his men together and they set off down the slope, following the bank of the Eden stream toward Cupar village in the warm noonday sunshine, thankful to be alive.

That evening the men who had come to fight for Knox and God's truth came back to St. Andrews. They crowded into the cathedral to worship and give thanks for their safety.

John Knox stepped into the high pulpit and looked down on them for a long time before he began to speak.

Then at last he said: "Beloved brethren, we have won a victory for God at Cupar Moor this day without a single blow being struck. Such is the mighty power of God when men stand up for him, even when they are afraid! Such is the power of the true kirk of Christ!

"It's true, we've only won a short truce. But one thing we must avoid, no matter how long or hard the coming fight may be. We must not hate these blind, wicked tyrants. Rather let us learn from Christ. Pray for your enemies, that the living God may snatch them as a brand out of the burning."

He did not preach long. When he was finished, the people bowed their heads in prayer.

"O God," prayed Master Knox, "mighty in wrath against thy foes, full of mercy to thy children: we praise thee for thy grace that moved thy faithful men to spring up in the night to fight for the true kirk. We bless thee that the mist at noon did lift to show a victory for thy cause. Grant, we beseech thee, that the day shall soon come when the dark mist of Rome shall lift from our land forever and we will see all Scotland won for the saving faith of Christ. In his holy name who is our Savior and Lord. Amen."

The people left the cathedral and went out into the dusk upon their homeward way. Rory Harris and his men of Crail marched wearily down the coast road from St. Andrews. They were too tired to sing. At every crossroad the Scottish folk cheered them as they passed, for the good news of Cupar Moor had spread across the land like a fire fanned by the wind.

"Last night," said Rory as he trudged along beside Malcolm "—was it only last night? I sat up late reading the Word of God before the fire and wearily went to bed."

Malcolm grunted. "Mistress Margaret won't have any trouble getting you to bed tonight."

"Aye," Rory chuckled. "As meek as my babes I'll be."

At last, as the moon rose in the crystal sky, the men of Crail stumbled into their village square. The women flocked out and found their husbands and fathers. The children, who should have been in bed, danced and sang around them. Silently the men took their families in their arms and were led away to their homes.

"Sweet Margaret," mumbled Rory, when his wife pulled the quilt up around his neck.

She smiled down at him and rubbed her fingers against his bristly cheek. "Sleep the blessed sleep of a faithful soldier of Christ," she whispered.

"I was afraid," muttered Rory. "My faith was weak. We may be beaten yet."

"God will still reign," replied his wife. "Good night, my love."

Scotland was quiet for the night. The mist began to blow in from the sea and shut away the stars. The land was dark and silent.

Wild Strawberries

UNDER THE DEEP BLUE of the bright June morning, Timothy and his dog, Jig, stood in the prow of the ship as they sailed up the main channel through Massachusetts Bay. When they were inside the shelter of some small islands they swung in toward Plum Cove. A seaman cast the sounding line and when the *Arbella* reached shallow water, the captain shouted a command.

"Drop anchors!"

With a rumble and a splash, the anchors plunged into the green water.

Timothy Miller grabbed Jig's front paws and danced wildly around in a circle on the deck. His mother and father and all the passengers on the ship were gathered at the railing to get their first good look at the new land which would be their home.

The ship was secured and the sails furled for a layover for the first time in almost nine weeks. Then the skiff was put over the side. The first load of passengers, mostly children and their parents, scrambled in and set off for the beach.

The instant the boat touched the shore, Timothy and his dog leaped out. The boy grinned as he saw bright-red flashes sparkling at the edge of the woods.

160

"Wild strawberries!" he cried. "Come on, Jig! Wild strawberries!" The boy and his dog, and the other children, set off on a run up the beach and into a clump of bushes.

Behind them, their parents were climbing out of the skiff. They were setting their feet on the dry land of New England for the first time. Some of them looked strangely pale. Many fell to their knees on the ground and thanked God once more for their safety and his protection during the long voyage across the North Atlantic.

The skiff pushed off and headed back out into Plum Cove, where the *Arbella* rode peacefully at anchor, for the next load of passengers waiting to come ashore. Ever since they had left England two months ago the *Arbella* had been their only home, her decks the only place they could exercise. They could hardly wait to stretch their legs ashore.

Through the warm summer afternoon, the people feasted on the wild strawberries. It was the first fresh food they had had, except for fish, since they had set sail. The children explored the nearby woods and ran up and down the beach. They shouted and laughed. They picked up sea shells and skipped flat stones across the waves. Then they scurried into the woods again for more strawberries.

Later all the people gathered on the beach and waited for the skiff to take them back to the *Arbella* for the night. The children were worn out with their

playing. Even Jig flopped on the ground and put his
nose on his front paws. He had no more strength to
chase the waves and snap at the scurrying crabs.

"Wild strawberries," sighed Timothy. He rubbed
his hand gently on his stomach and grinned up at his
father. "I'm glad the Lord called us to New England."

"Wild strawberries or not," answered his father,
"here we can serve God as he requires in the Scrip-

tures, and build up a nation worthy of the Lord."
He looked off at the strange wooded hills. "It'll
take more than gathering wild strawberries, I fear."

The wooded hills of the countryside around the bay
were not strange for long. During the summer months
that followed, many ships brought English families
across the Atlantic to begin life anew in the Bay
Colony.

John and Sarah Miller and their son, Timothy,
went with a group of families to live in the little settlement which they called Boston. They built a log hut
and a small shed under a wooded knoll. Timothy and
his father cleared a patch of ground around their new
home for a garden and planted a few vegetables. But
it was too late in the year for much to grow.

Timothy roamed the gently rolling countryside
with Jig, exploring the brooks that splashed into the
bay. He carried water from the spring on the knoll
for his mother and chopped kindling for the fire.

The days grew shorter. The leaves on the trees turned yellow and red and brown, and began to fall. The nights got cold. And then the settlers began to get sick. There were no more wild berries or nuts to find in the woods. The wild radishes and onions were gone. The people had to eat the hardtack and salt meat left from the ships that had brought them so far from England.

One evening Timothy's father came into their hut and set his ax by the doorway.

"'Tis a rugged, barren land," he muttered. He slumped down on the dirt floor and held out his hands to warm them over the fire. "Four months now I've been working to clear this land of ours. Three hundred trees I've cut down, if I've cut down one." He turned his hands and looked at the calluses and cracks on them. "Stumps pulled out by the score. Bushels of brush and nettles."

"Here, John," said his wife, handing him a mug of tea, "this will warm you up."

"Wh-ff!" he gasped when he had tasted the tea. "Woman, what's this awful stuff?"

"It's birchbark tea," she answered.

"Turpentine, you mean," he muttered. "I'd rather drink water than that—or even 'drink of the wrath of the Almighty.' "

His wife laughed. "Drink it anyway," she replied. "The warmth will keep away the fever from your bones." She came and stood behind him, looking into the fire. She put her hands on his shoulders. "I must

not lose you, my husband. Oh, how I pray the winter
will not carry us all away to the grave."

John Miller reached up and took her hand. "I'll
drink this witch's brew then, my sweet. It will keep
even the devil away. And where is Timothy?"

"He should be home before long," she answered.
"He went off with the Sanders boys to hunt for clams
and mussels in the tidal rocks."

"Humph," said the man. "Hardtack and salt beef.

Birchbark tea. And now clams and mussels. And three months until spring! Do you know what we'd be eating if we were back in England now?"

"Hush," his wife said. "'Man doth not live by bread only.'"

"Aye. It was only a thought," answered the man, with a smile. "It is far better to starve in New England, if God wills, and serve him in purity of faith."

At that moment Timothy burst in through the door flap.

"The Lord was good to us!" he said excitedly. "Look!" He tipped up his bag and dumped a pile of clams and mussels out by the fire. "And here!" he cried. He pulled out a small perch. "I caught him! He was trapped in a tidal pool!"

Timothy's father looked at the pile of clams and mussels. He took the fish and held it in front of him by its sticky tail. "The Lord will provide," he sighed. "Praise be to God our provider. But we'll all die of scurvy and starvation yet, if a ship doesn't get to us from old England soon!"

On Christmas Eve a bitter cold descended on the colony. Next morning, Timothy rolled over stiffly in his ragged blanket and opened his eyes. Jig was curled up at his feet, wheezing in his sleep. The hut was cold and dark. A crack of early morning light seeped in around the door flap. Then he heard it! Footsteps crept past outside.

Indians! he thought. Jig heard it too. He opened his eyes and perked up his ears. "Father," whispered Timothy. "Indians outside!"

His father mumbled restlessly in his sleep but did not wake up. Timothy crept out of his blanket and crawled painfully to the door flap on hands and knees. What he saw was worse than Indians. Two men, neighbor Sanders and his brother, were slowly carrying a shrouded body up the path toward King's Chapel, as they called the little log meetinghouse. Timothy watched them until they disappeared into the woods. He shivered and turned back into the hut. Then he noticed for the first time that his mother was not there. Her blanket was folded on the stool.

"Father!" he cried. "Wake up!"

"Wha—what?" his father answered. He sat up and blinked.

"Mother's gone!" the boy cried.

"Gone?" his father repeated. "Is it morning already?"

"But she's gone!" Timothy repeated.

"Aye," his father said. He stood up and stretched. "Br-r-r," he gritted. "It's been a long night for her, likely enough. Eli Sanders came at midnight. I guess his wife's sick with the fever." He leaned over to pick up his boots and pulled them on with a groan.

"Mrs. Sanders?" Timothy asked. "But—but I just saw them on the path to King's Chapel. Mr. Sanders and his brother."

Just then Timothy's mother pushed the door flap aside and came into the hut. She stood there wearily with her eyes closed.

"Sarah," his father said. "Poor Sarah. You've been up all night."

She looked up at him. Tears came into her eyes.

"Here, now," he said. He stepped over and put his arms around her. "You're very tired. Hold fast, my sweet one, hold fast. Timothy, go get some kindling for the fire."

Timothy and Jig pushed through the door flap and stumbled out into the icy Christmas morning. Across the narrow valley on the edge of the woods he could see the bark wigwam of the Sanders family.

He scuffed along up the path. In spite of all he could do, he began to cry. The Sanders boys were his best friends. What would they do now, without their mother?

By the stack of kindling he saw the dried-up leaves of a strawberry plant. "Wild strawberries," he muttered to himself, remembering the first day when they had landed in the bay. It seemed a very long time ago. He pulled his coat closer around his neck. His fingers burned with the bitter cold as he tried to pick up some sticks of kindling wood. On his way back it began to snow. Grainy ice crystals poured down like frozen sand.

The next day Timothy and his parents trudged wearily through the fine snow to King's Chapel. There they gathered with the rest of the families of the Boston settlement for Mrs. Sanders' funeral.

In the icy chill of the bare room they listened to the minister read the words of Holy Scripture. Timothy huddled in his threadbare coat and tried to keep his teeth from chattering. But the fierce cold and the grief of his friends, the Sanders boys, made him shiver. He felt sick and his back ached. Now and then he caught the words the minister was reading.

" '. . . No condemnation to them which are in Christ Jesus. . . . The Spirit beareth witness with our spirits that we are the children of God . . . joint heirs with Christ; if so be that we suffer with him. . . . The sufferings of this present time are not worthy to be compared with the glory which shall be revealed in us. . . . O grave, where is thy victory? . . . But thanks be to God, which giveth us the victory through our Lord Jesus Christ. . . .' "

The service did not last long—only an hour instead of the usual two. It was too cold for the people to stay and talk as they used to do. Quietly they greeted each other, trying to smile. They did not say much, for they knew one another too well to need words. They shook Eli Sanders' hand or pressed his shoulder to show their friendship and affection. Then they turned silently away and went homeward in the snow, wondering which of them the Lord would call next. They knew that many more of them would weaken and die of the bitter cold and starvation if the *Lion* did not soon get back from England with food and supplies.

It seemed as if the snowstorms would never end. During one of the wildest blizzards of all, Timothy's father straggled into their hut. His fingers were frostbitten and too weak to hold his ax. He let it drop and fell before the fire.

"No use," he groaned. "God forgive me." He coughed and pressed his hand against his sore mouth.

He lay there trembling, with his drawn face buried in his arms.

Timothy sat huddled in his thin blankets, staring into the small fire. Jig lay very still on his lap, too weak to do more than crawl in and out of the hut.

Timothy's father rolled over with a groan. "Sarah," he said. There was no answer. "Sarah?" He sat up suddenly, forgetting the soreness in his joints. "Timothy, where's your mother?"

Timothy stared dully into the fire. "Getting some wood," he mumbled. He began to cry. Jig did not move.

"Where?" demanded his father. "I didn't see her! Where is she, boy?"

Timothy tried to speak. He opened his mouth, but he only gagged. His father stared at him in horror.

"Timothy!" he cried. "No! Don't, Timothy! Don't cry!" He jumped up like a madman. "O God," he cried, "save us and deliver us! Don't let my little boy starve! Don't cry, Timothy, I'll be back. I'll get us some food somewhere." He whirled and rushed out through the door flap. "Sarah! Sarah!" he called, as he ran off down the path.

Timothy closed his eyes and slumped over next to the fire. Jig crawled in close under his arm. He whimpered and flicked Timothy's nose with his warm, red tongue. "Jig," the boy mumbled. "Good dog. . . . See—the wild strawberries. . . ." His arm went limp.

The next thing Timothy knew, he began to feel warm. He felt as if he were floating in space. Far away he could hear tinkling sounds. And then, as he began to listen, the tinkling began to sound like people laughing. In his sleep he smiled.

"That's it, Timothy," he seemed to hear his mother say. "Come on, wake up. It's all right, Timothy. Open your eyes, Timothy."

He felt something being pushed against his mouth, something cold and wet. He pulled his head away.

"Drink it, silly boy. Oh, Timothy," his mother was laughing, "open your eyes and see!"

He felt himself being shaken gently. At last he tried to open his eyes. He could make out a roaring fire. He was being held in his father's arms.

"M-mother?" he whispered.

"Oh, the Lord be praised," said his mother gently. "Here, now, open your mouth and take a sip."

He saw that she had a cup in her hand. She held it up to his lips. He made a face, for it tasted sour. He could hardly swallow it.

"Hooray!" Timothy heard. Curiously, he looked around. Standing there about the roaring fire he saw the Sanders boys and their father.

"Hi, Timothy!" one of the boys said. "Drink it! It's lemon juice! Tastes real good!" Each boy had a cup in his hand. "Bet we can drink ours faster'n you!"

Timothy smiled weakly. He forgot how sore his mouth was. He took the cup from his mother with shaking hands and guzzled the lemon juice down. It was so sour it made his eyes water, but he drained the last drop from the cup without taking a breath.

"Whew!" he whispered.

The Sanders boys grinned at him. "Try it again. There's plenty more! The *Lion* just sailed in from England with supplies!"

"The *Lion*?" Timothy asked. "Food?"

His mother smiled. "Everything is going to be all right now," she said. "Soon we'll all be well. The Lord has been gracious and kind. He has not forgotten his people."

Timothy's father set him back on his blanket by the fire, with another cup of lemon juice.

Just then the door flap was pushed open and a stalwart seaman from the *Lion* came into the hut. He was snow-covered, sweating, and laughing. Under one arm he carried a sack of grain and under the other a bag of dried beans.

"Here's some grub to fill the hollows of your soul!" he laughed, setting the food down by the fire. "And down at the landing's a plow and half a barrel of beef for you!" He looked at John Miller and Eli Sanders. "Think you're well enough to carry 'em back?"

The two colonists looked at each other.

" 'The Lord is my strength and my shield,' " said Timothy's father. "Come on, Eli Sanders, let's go and get that plow!"

175

Eli looked at him carefully. "But, John," he said, "didn't you swear last week you were taking the first ship back to England?"

Timothy's father drew up to his full height, forgetting the soreness of his body. "I did not swear to it," he replied. "But may the Lord forgive my cowardice for even thinking it! True, my faith faltered, but now I only want that plow and we shall stay! 'No man, having put his hand to the plow and looking back, is fit for the kingdom of God.'"

Timothy sat on the blanket drinking his lemon juice. Jig crawled into his lap and licked his chin wherever the lemon juice spilled.

"Good," said Timothy to the Sanders boys. "Now when the summer comes, I'll be here with you for the wild strawberries!"

All Hail the Power of Jesus' Name!

Button McKeever rolled over on the dirt floor and blinked his eyes. He lay sprawled under a bench. The tavern was silent now, although it was the noisiest den of thieves and murderers in all of Rogues Harbor. Silence meant danger in that part of Kentucky.

He rubbed his dirty face and sat up. Then he heard the noise. The whole gang of men were out in the road shouting and swearing, and the dust was flying.

"Diggety!" Button groaned. "A fight."

He weaved to his feet and staggered to the door just in time to see the tavernkeeper knocked flat in the dust by a stranger.

"Ow!" gasped Button, for the tavernkeeper was the toughest, dirtiest fighter in that part of the mountains. The mob roared and cheered. Suddenly they were on the stranger's side—at least until the fight was over! Any man who could beat up the tavernkeeper deserved respect.

Then the strangest thing happened that Button or any of them had ever seen. They stopped shouting, even closed their mouths. There was the stranger, as big a man as ever rode into Rogues Harbor, sitting on the tavernkeeper and singing at the top of his lungs. That in itself was not strange, but it was the song!

"All Hail the Power of Jesus' Name!" he was sing-ing, keeping time by banging the tavernkeeper's head in the dirt. The singing and banging went on and on for three stanzas! Finally the tavernkeeper gave up.

"All right!" he gasped. "'Nough—'nough!"

The big stranger grinned and shouted, "Amen, brother!" He stood up and lifted the dazed, dusty tavernkeeper to his feet.

"Now, good friend," said the stranger, "you keep your promise, or I'll sing all five stanzas next time. You and your friends here leave us preachers alone after this. The gospel of Christ will be preached in Logan County and all over Kentucky. You and your kind stay out of the way, or come and hear the gospel peacefully. And if you ever want to look me up, the name is Reverend Peter Cartwright!"

The stranger's shoulders were too broad, his eyes were too deep and flashing, for anybody to take a chance on disagreeing. He swung up on his black horse and grinned down at the silent, scowling tavern-keeper. The crowd of men stared in awe as the preacher flicked his reins and slowly sauntered off up the road, singing at the top of his voice: " 'All hail the power of Jesus' Name! Let angels prostrate fall.' "

Button frowned deeply and rubbed his beardless chin. Back to the table. Back to the jug, he thought to himself.

The men swarmed into the tavern, laughing and swearing.

"There's one preacher we'll have to fix right!" sneered Bloody James Alder, the gambler. "Wait till some dark night! I'll slit his croaking gullet and send his tongue in a tiny pine box to his bishop!" The mob roared with laughter. The tavernkeeper held his head.

"You and who else?" Button said quietly. The crowd looked around.

"Oh?" sneered Bloody James. "Has the drunken child awoken?" He pushed his way through the men and shook a fist in Button's face. "You smelly little scorpion! Want a knife in your gizzard too, is that it?"

Button's eyes were cool and steady, for this sort of thing sharpened his senses. He had only been in the Rogues Harbor country for a month. He was a small youth, only eighteen, but he was as tough and wiry as a hungry mountain lion. Without a flicker of an eyelid he stared Bloody James down. Then with a grip of steel he grabbed the gambler's wrist and twisted. The man's sneer turned instantly to fright and pain.

"How many men have you killed, Bloody?" Button's words were cool, almost friendly.

"All right! All right!" cried the gambler in panic. The crowd laughed, for everybody there knew that Bloody James was only a smalltime crooked gambler. He had never killed anybody!

"Well, son," a big man called Scalper grinned at Button, "seein' how you don't care to have the preacher's throat slit, what else you got in mind?"

Button looked around at the crowd. "Scalper," he answered, "just between you and me, I have an idea."

"You heard the boy," Scalper said to the others. "Git!" The men turned away, muttering to themselves. "Now," said Scalper, "you're a smart young Bostonian. What's your idea?"

"Well, it's this," Button replied. "You ever been to one of those camp meetings?"

"Camp meetings!" Scalper said. "Now, look here, boy—"

"Hold on," grinned Button. "I didn't ask were you converted."

"I ain't goin' within ten miles of no hollerin', stompin', white-o'-your-eyes camp meetin'!" bellowed Scalper.

The whole crowd of thieves looked around and stared.

"Look out there, Scalper," one of them shouted. "Maybe Button's tryin' to save yore immortal soul!" The men guffawed.

Scalper glared at them and they stopped laughing. "All right, now, sonny, what're you talking about?"

"I'm just saying there's lots of people loose around camp meetings, plenty to steal. All we have to do is watch our chances and take what we want. Get that big preacher and his pals going loud and strong, and nobody'll pay us any notice!"

Scalper sat back. "Aw," he said, "that ain't hardly fair. 'Taint right to go stealin' from folks when they're hearin' the word o' God!" He began to smile slyly.

"By gum, we'll let the preachers come. Like that Cartwright feller tells us, we'll sure leave 'em alone! Why, you know, down there at Cane Ridge couple years ago was a crowd—they say there was twenty thousand folks there for a whole week! Even I couldn't rob that many people one at a time if I had ten years to do it in!"

He stood up and looked over the crowd of thieves and robbers and murderers in the tavern. "Now listen here, you dirty sinners!" he shouted. "What's needed in Rogues Harbor is some real religion!" They frowned and blinked. "Button, here, is the smartest thief we've had in these mountains fer years. And what he's thought up is goin' to change our way o' thievin' for a while! Now, listen. Here's what we're goin' to do. . . ."

Not long after that the annual Mud River camp meeting gathered. Wagonloads of people from miles around flocked to the clearing along the river. There were rich people and poor people, farmers, merchants, doctors, preachers, saints and sinners, young people and old, children and hobbling grandfathers.

Long lines of tents stretched off into the forest on every side, with thousands of excited people hustling about.

Bloody James Alder and part of the mob from Rogues Harbor pitched their tents on the far north side of the camp, deep among the pines. Scalper and some of the others, with clean linen and trimmed whiskers, found their places on the opposite side. They too, having arrived late, pitched their tents at a long distance from the clearing. But they did not mind having to walk past some five hundred other tents to get down to the river.

Button McKeever and the rest of the thieves from the Harbor found other places on the fringe of the camp. They sighed wearily, but they assured the little old lady down the line that they would be happy enough to walk all that way to the distant river— even run, if the Spirit moved them!

That night the Harbor men mingled with the crowds. They practiced a little petty pickpocketing to tune up their fingers. They wandered through the gatherings, getting in mind the layout of the camp.

Great campfires blazed in the clearing by the river and back in the fringe woods of the forest. The long lines of tents seemed to march back into the endless depths of the silent forest, until they were lost in the dark night under the trees. Hundreds of candles and lamps staggered and danced in the evening breeze. Torches billowed fiery smoke and made the ancient shadow spirits of the forest lurk and leap. Groups of campers gathered around the campfires. Their singing filled the darkness, swelling and falling on the wind of the night.

Already in the first evening, preachers were beginning to raise their voices for God's moving Spirit to come down and convict their hearers of sin. Earnest prayers soared into the trees. It did not take long for many of the campers to get in the mood. They had been looking forward to this camp meeting through long months. There was no time left for sleep now, until salvation came!

The next day the preachers and listeners got into full swing. People soon began to be moved by their

excitement. Rich and poor, dignified and unmannered, scoffers and believers, they reacted to the pleas of the preachers. Stricken sinners began to roll on the ground. Some ran screaming through the clearing and into the river. Many who would be standing soberly one moment would suddenly stiffen as if they had been turned to stone, and fall like logs to the ground.

During the early hours of the second evening, the Harbor brethren met by themselves quite far out in the forest. They went beyond the glare of the blazing fires and beyond the incessant noise of hoarse hymn-singing and shrieking.

"I've had enough, Button," growled Scalper. "My nerves are getting jumpy."

"Come on, Button," whined Bloody James, "let's get it over with."

All the men agreed. So far, they had been able to stay on the fringes.

"What if one of us catches it?" they whispered.

"Then I'll shoot him," snarled Scalper.

That took care of that. They set their plans. At midnight, when the main camp bell rang the hour, the three wings of the robber band would go into action.

"Don't kill anybody," ordered Scalper. "No need to scare people! Just take what's handy and then clear out fast. There'll be plenty for all, a harvest such as we've never had before! Half of you get ready to break camp. The other half does the stealing. But fast, now! We'll divide the loot when we get back to Rogues Harbor."

The men split up and drifted back into the camp unnoticed as the evening grew late. Button and Scalper finally strolled into the clearing and joined the congregation that was nearest to the camp bell.

"How long?" whispered Button.

Scalper shrugged. "Don't know. Half hour. Fifteen minutes. This watch I stole last night—I can't wind it."

They stood nervously on the edge of the crowd as the moments passed. The preacher was shouting at a fevered pitch. People were falling to their knees here and there.

"Hey, Button, come on," Scalper whispered hoarsely. "There's the feller that rings the bell. It's time to go!"

Button turned around and stared at Scalper. His face suddenly went white. "No!" he gasped. Just as the man struck the bell for midnight, he staggered back. His eyes grew wide with sick horror and panic.

Scalper stared in amazement. "Button!" he cried. But it was too late. Button threw his hands up to his face and fell over.

"Button—" gasped Scalper.

Already eager onlookers were gathering around. "Pray, brother!" they cried. "Confess your sins!"

Scalper ran away into the night as fast as he could go, and he did not stop until he was far up the trail toward the wilderness.

When Button opened his eyes it was morning, and an old woman was kneeling by his side praying. He could not recall where he was. He did not know the old woman.

Then the sound of singing came to his buzzing ears. A hymn! It came from quite a distance away. When

187

he was a little boy the singing across the yard at the church used to sound like that. His mother would put him to bed for the night and then go over to the church with his father, the minister.

"Are you awake, son?" asked the old woman. "I'm glad you woke up now. Took you a long time. Lots longer than most."

"What happened?" Button asked. He looked up at the pine trees. Nothing seemed to mean anything.

"What's your name, boy?" asked the old woman.

"Bertram. Bertram—" The name sounded strange to him. He sat up suddenly and stared at the old woman. "Button!" he said. A cold chill swept over him.

"It's all right, son," murmured the old woman. She struggled to get to her feet. "Praise the Lord!" she sighed. "You just lie back a spell. I'll get you a minister."

He fell back to the ground and rolled over. All the wickedness of his soul swept over him. All his fighting and stealing and lying sprang before his mind's eye. Everything at once swarmed over him, from the time four years before when he had run away from his Massachusetts home, down the long, bloody, ugly trail to New Orleans and then to Rogues Harbor.

"O God," he groaned, "I can never be forgiven! O Lord, save me!"

All the beatings and whippings his father had given him flooded back into his mind. "Do right. Do right,

Bertram! Obey God's commandments. Do what you're told! You're headed for hell, Bertram! *For hell*, Bertram!"

Finally a big, broad-shouldered preacher came and knelt by his side under the pine tree. Button looked up at him, weeping. It was Peter Cartwright!

"Beloved," said the preacher, "look up now. The Lord knows your sins. He knows how dirty your soul is and how much you need to be forgiven. But praise him, son. Thank your Lord for his great mercy. Not by your own goodness but by his blessed Son's cross and blood you are saved. Come on, now. Kneel here with me. Hold my hand while we go before the glorious throne of grace."

Button crawled to his knees and reached out blindly. When he felt the big preacher's hand he grasped it tightly. The prayer was simple and short. Then it was quiet.

As Button searched his own heart, the whole world slowly began to open up. He began to see the passing faces of his companions—Scalper, Bloody James, and all the others he had known in his wanderings, and all the people he had robbed and frightened and hurt. And then he saw a vast, unnumbered multitude of strange faces, millions and millions, all lost and wandering the earth, dying alone, just as he was himself. Lost and afraid and alone.

He felt heavy and very sick inside. "O God," he wept in his soul, "save us! Bring us home!"

For a long time he lay still on the ground. The big preacher knelt in silent prayer near him. The breeze was sighing through the pines. He felt he could never move again unless God came and took him.

And then it happened, in one instant, like the sunlight suddenly pouring into a dark, windowless room when the door opens. He looked up and stared in front of him.

"Me, Lord? But I— *I can't!* I—"

He sat up, frowning and thinking hard. "Go ye, therefore, and teach all nations," he murmured to himself.

Three months later and a thousand miles northeast of Mud River, Button walked into a village inn near Williams College with a Bible under his arm.

"Well," crowed a drunken college student, "look who jus' walked in the door! Williams' newest son!" He leered dizzily at the newcomer. Six other students were sitting at the table in the low, smoke-filled room. "Here's a lad needs his first lesson!" the student went on. "Came to college for that, didn't you, boy?" His friends snickered and looked knowingly at one another.

Button's eyes were cool and steady, for threats always sharpened his senses.

"Well, fraidy-cat," snarled the drunken student, "speak up when you're spoken to by y'r betters! We're jus' liable to smear that little beardless face o'

yours in the gutter outside!" He looked around at his grinning companions. "Maybe even get that purty little boy's brand-new suit all dirty! Tsk! Tsk! Tsk!" They snickered and snorted.

Button stepped toward them, smiling. He didn't mind a little friendly jesting.

"Hey!" shouted the student angrily. "Where you think you're going? This is f'r seniors only. Whisky's not for children!" He blinked as he saw the Bible under Button's arm. "Why, do tell!" he smirked. "I b'lieve a Christian has come to save our lost, immortal souls!"

191

His friends guffawed and hooted. "Go on! Get out! We'll take care o' you later! Beat it, preacher!" His companions giggled.

Without a flicker of an eyelid, Button gazed at them. He did not move. Now he was not smiling.

"Say," growled the student, "guess you ain't got no gentlemanly manners! Guess I'll hafta—"

But he never had a chance to finish the sentence. Button had put his Bible down on an empty table. Now suddenly he was on them, knocking their pewter beer mugs flying. He tipped the table over on them. There was a mad scramble. The room filled with sudden cries of pain. Faces went white and noses bled and eyes stared in panic as Button tore into them with all the skill of a frontier outlaw. Those who could, fled. The others lay on the floor, stunned sober by the violent attack.

"Now," said Button quietly, pushing his hair out of his eyes, "it's time for a little lesson, as you said." He gazed at them. "Sit up!" The youths cowered. "I said, sit up!" Button reached under his coat and pulled out a knife whose flashing blade had seen more serious work. The students gasped and sat up. "Now," said Button, "we'll have a little singing lesson, and you better sing while you've got your throats!"

He straightened up and began to sing. " 'All hail the power of Jesus' Name! Let angels prostrate fall; Bring forth the royal diadem . . . ' "

When the innkeeper came into the room he was startled and puzzled. There were his noisiest young customers sitting all bloodied up on the floor amongst the wreckage of chairs and tables. And they were singing a hymn at the top of their voices while a young stranger beat the time with a long, flashing knife.

One Saturday afternoon in August, three years later, Button McKeever packed his bag. Several of his young Christian friends were with him in his room. They were members of a secret student society called simply "The Brethren."

"But, listen," said one of them. "Why won't you stay for just a few more months?"

Button smiled as he tried to fold his one linen shirt. "I'll miss our prayer meetings, Samuel," he answered. He could not look at them, for he felt his throat getting tight. He did not want to break down in front of them. "I'll—I'll miss having friends like you. And the long bull sessions all the way to the dawn! And the good singing. But the praying, most of all."

"That's just what we think," Samuel answered. "So stay with us. Go on to seminary with us. There's a lot more to learn."

Button shook his head. "I don't need any more education where I'm going," he said. "I've got what I came back for. Out west people need the Bible and they need preachers. Maybe later, someday, they'll

need real scholars too." He grinned. "Then you can come out! 'Doctor Samuel J. Mills, Professor of Theology'!"

"But in another few months," Samuel objected, "you would graduate."

Button shrugged. "Brethren of the society," he said, "remember last year out at the haystack? Samuel, you said we ought to send the gospel to all the dark and heathen lands—Africa, India, China, the whole world—and you said we could do it if we would. Well, God willing, we can! Every place on

earth there are people dying for want of the gospel.
I've got to go to the people I know best, so I'm going
back to the Rogues Harbor country and the valley of
the Mississippi. I got most of my education out there
before I ever came to school!"

He picked up his bag and looked around the room
one last time. "All right, I guess I'm ready."

The Brethren went with him down to the farm
where he kept his horse. A summer thunderstorm
was gathering and the air was hot and still.

"We'll always pray for you," said Samuel, as But-

195

ton swung up into the saddle. "The Lord be with you till we meet again."

"Amen," Button said. He waved to his friends and spurred the horse into a trot, as the first crack of thunder flashed through the heavy black clouds. "Till we meet again!" he called.

His heart pounded as he turned west on the road. This was the moment he had been working and waiting for since that morning at Mud River. Tears glistened in his eyes. "Lord Jesus Christ," he whispered, "use me. Speak thy word through me. Let me burn myself out for thy gospel, if only the saving light of God may shine forth all the way to the Mississippi!"

The rain began to come down in big drops, kicking up the powdery dust of the road in little puffs.

"Look out, Scalper—Bloody James—Rogues Harbor. I'm coming back with your share of the heavenly treasure!"

The fields smelled clean and fresh in the summer rain. The thunder blasted and rolled and filled the black sky like the very voice of God. A farmer looked out of his barn door and scratched his head in wonder when he saw the young man riding past on the road in the heavy downpour, singing at the top of his voice—
" *'All hail the power of Jesus' Name! Let angels prostrate fall. . . .'* "

The Wind Tower

Uncle Willie shuffled slowly across the moonlit compound after finishing his regular night check of the wards. There were not many patients any more. None of the Chinese wanted to come to a Christian hospital or to be treated by an American doctor. After all, the newspapers carried stories every day about missionaries whom the Communist Government arrested and accused of being spies and enemy agents.

Uncle Willie shook his head sadly as he went up the gravel path. Twenty-five years ago he had helped to build the hospital. He had given his whole life to the people of the Szechwan plain. They were his friends. The dearest of them were his fellow Christians. They loved him enough to call him "Uncle Willie."

When he got to his cottage he stopped at the gate and looked back down the slope. The bright spring moonlight shone on the tiled roof of Tapaing Hospital and flooded the valley below with silver light. He could see the faint, dark line of the river that flowed away into the night, southward across the plain for two hundred miles until it poured into the great Yangtze.

Ten thousand times before he had stood on this very spot by his gate looking out over that beautiful, peaceful sight. But now he sighed wearily and went into the house. It was all over. The rest of the missionary staff had already left months ago, while they still had a chance to get out of China. But his heart would not let him go with them. Now in another two weeks the deadline for the next month's tax would go by. The hospital would not be able to pay. The communists would come in and take over. The wards and halls of Christ's hospital in the Tapaing foothills would echo with communist songs and political lectures. The Lord of life would be scorned, laughed at, perhaps in time even forgotten.

He got into his pajamas and knelt by his bed, but

it was hard to pray. Twenty-five years of love and sacrifice for Christ were being swept aside. In the past three months many of the fellow Christians he loved had been dragged away to prison or hauled out to the fields to be shot.

He got up from his knees and into bed. He lay on his back staring at the ceiling in the dark. "O God," he groaned, "help me to trust thee."

Sometime late in the night he woke up from a dead sleep. The back of his neck crawled with the shock of surprise and fear, for a Chinese police officer was shaking him by the shoulder.

"Dr. LaForce," the officer was saying, "you are under arrest."

"Wha—why?" gasped Uncle Willie.

"Come," repeated the officer. "Get up. You are to come with us to the village police station."

Uncle Willie rose up on his elbows and looked around. Six soldiers stood in a line inside the door. He climbed out of bed, trembling with the shock of being awakened so suddenly out of a heavy sleep. As he pulled on his clothes the soldiers stood impassively, with their rifles on their shoulders. He got his sleeping bag and his Bible. Then they marched him out of the house and down the path past the hospital in the middle of the night.

At the village police station, he was taken into a small, bare courtroom. The local People's Commissar sat at the table with a stack of papers before him.

"What is your name and where are you from?" he asked.

"I am Dr. Wilbur LaForce from the Tapaing Hospital," answered Uncle Willie.

"You are a liar, Dr. LaForce," said the commissar coldly. "You are from the United States. You are a spy for the warmongering Americans, the cruel enemies of the peaceful Chinese People's Republic!"

"Rot!" snorted Uncle Willie. "You know better than that, Li-Ting! You've known me ever since you were a little boy."

"Silence!" snapped the commissar. "You are a capitalist spy! Do you think we don't know all about you?" He tapped the pile of papers on the table. "Here is proof, evil doctor, that you have betrayed

the Chinese people, who were stupid enough to believe you came to help them!"

Uncle Willie's eyes flashed with anger. "I just
took the stitches out of your stomach two months
ago, Li-Ting! Was that betrayal?"

"A simple way to fool us, Dr. LaForce. But we are
not fools. You cannot buy the Chinese people!"

Uncle Willie stared at him in amazement. "Have
I spent twenty-five years ministering to the bodies

and souls of people for whom Christ died and rose again, just to fool you all? You're just plain crazy, Li-Ting—blind and crazy!"

"Go on, Doctor," replied the commissar smoothly. "What other lies and insults will you add to this pile of evidence?"

"Evidence? Trash! You have nothing at all against me, and you know it!" Uncle Willie said. "Who built Tapaing Hospital for you? Who paid for the surgical instruments? Who sent the medicine and the drugs that have healed and comforted you and your father and mother and the rest of the village, Li-Ting, ever since you were a schoolboy? Who built the school for you? Who paid the professors who came to teach you at Nanking University?"

"American imperialists, Dr. LaForce," sneered the commissar.

"Christians!" shouted the doctor.

"Capitalist swine! American imperialists who would steal China for themselves and make us slaves!" Li-Ting spat out the words.

"Christians!" shouted Uncle Willie, even louder. "Americans, yes, but American *Christians!* People who sent their money and gave their lives for Christ and his gospel, and for nothing else! For Christ's Kingdom and no other cause! For Christ, the true Son of God, whom you yourself once called your Lord and Savior, Li-Ting."

"Silence!" ordered the commissar. His face was

red and wet with perspiration. "Take him away! Take the wicked spy out of here!" He glared at the doctor. "You will pay dearly for your treason to the people of China, Dr. LaForce."

Uncle Willie looked at Li-Ting. He sighed. "Forgive me, my son," he said quietly. "Two years ago I could never have believed that I would stand in this room before you—you, of all people—and hear you say these lies. May the Lord Jesus Christ forgive your treason against his eternal Kingdom."

"Get out!" screamed Li-Ting, rising suddenly and knocking his chair over. He shook his fist at Uncle Willie. His lips trembled and his eyes stared wildly.

"Good-by, Li-Ting," said the doctor as the guards led him away. "Thank the Lord Jesus that your Christian father is not alive to see what has happened to you."

In the lonely weeks that followed, the doctor sat by the hour reading his Bible, memorizing passages of Scripture as fast as he could. Soon they might take the Bible away from him, and he would have to keep his faith alive and strong with only the remembered word of God.

Some of the time during the long, silent days and nights he stood on his stool and looked out of the high window. He could see the roof of the hospital. His heart longed to be back there, for it was his home. Then one day the guard caught him standing by the window and took his stool away from him so that he

could not see anything but the blue sky in the day-
time and a few stars at night. He had left his Bible
on the table by mistake. They took that too.

One morning in the middle of the summer, four
months after they arrested him, he was taken out of
the jail. They let him go back to his house with an
armed guard, so he could gather a few clothes together. He slipped a small New Testament into his
pants pocket unnoticed. Then they took him back
down to the village and put him on the old train that
passed through every other day.

"You are being sent to Chungking, spy," said Li-
Ting. "You will be given the justice you deserve."

Uncle Willie could not answer Li-Ting; his spirit was too full of sadness and sorrow. As the train wheezed and jerked and clanked out of the village, he caught one last glimpse of the hospital on the hill. Tears came to his eyes, for he never expected to see it again.

But the train did not take Uncle Willie to Chungking, after all. When it arrived in Chengtu that evening, the coach was shunted off on a siding for the night. The prisoners were given no food or water. They were not allowed to get out of the car or even stand up and stretch. Guards surrounded the coach outside.

Early the next morning, Uncle Willie and some of the others were transferred to an Army truck. The canvas canopy and the tail flap were tied down. They could not see out, but sat in the dark. The sun got higher and the summer heat became almost unbearable, with no water to drink, as the truck drove for hours over a rough, steep road. They were not going south toward Chungking at all! They must be going west into the wild, desolate mountains along the borders of Tibet!

Once Uncle Willie tried to start some kind of conversation with the other prisoners to break the silence and lonely fear that seemed to grip them all.

"Are any of you Christians?" he asked. One or two looked over at him. He could not tell whether they meant that they were, or if they were only startled at the sound of a voice.

Then one of the prisoners in the far corner spoke up. "Christian! Bah! Barbarious superstition!" Uncle Willie did not answer. The speaker might not be a real prisoner at all. It would be wiser to keep quiet for the time being at least.

All day long the truck wound its way through mountains. The prisoners suffered in ever greater misery as their thirst grew. In the cramped space no one could move or stretch, and their legs and arms ached with stiffness. Several of the men sprawled on the floor of the truck bed, groaning in pain. One of them seemed to be dying, but there was no way to help him. The doctor could only sit and watch. It was horrible not to be able to help.

Late in the afternoon the truck at last came to a halt. The tail flap was unlocked and the prisoners were ordered to get out. Several collapsed on the ground and had to be kicked by some soldiers before they struggled to their feet. They found themselves on a rock shelf a few hundred feet across. An ancient fortress prison stood before them. It looked very small compared to the wild, barren mountains that towered around it in sheer cliffs. Fifty feet from the road the narrow shelf dropped away into a steep gorge, and a swift mountain stream rushed down along the bottom.

"The Upper Yalung, I think," mumbled one of the prisoners. "No one escapes from this place."

At the moment, Uncle Willie did not care much. At least he was free to stand up and stretch. The wind blowing up through the canyon felt fresh and good to him, after thirty-six hours of foul air and cramped misery in the train coach and the truck.

The guards soon had the prisoners lined up. Uncle Willie got a final glimpse of the open mountains and the wild, free Yalung River before he was marched with the others through the fortress gate. It was the last time he would see free, open space for two long years.

The good doctor spent the next eighteen months in Yalung Prison. Most of the time he spent in a cell alone, although now and then he would have a roommate for a month or two. His cell was eleven feet long and seven feet wide, with a high ceiling. The window at the end of the narrow room was covered over with heavy paper so that he could not look out. Above it were two small windows which were always open for air and a little light. He could see just a little pie-shaped piece of the sky through each of them. One day he found that if he pressed against the corner of his cell and stood on his toes he could see a very small part of the mountain ridge across the canyon. A single bulb in the ceiling was the only light he had.

A table and a stool in his cell were bolted to the floor. He rolled his sleeping bag out on a bamboo rack set upon two old pine boxes which had once been used to ship Washington apples from Wenatchee.

The guards who watched over the doctor refused to take his messages to the prison officials. "They will talk to you when they choose, foreign spy," his guards would answer. He paced back and forth in his narrow

cell to keep from getting stiff and cramped. But his
heart was heavy.

Nothing lies ahead for me but prison and torture
and death, he thought. What have I done to deserve
this?

One night during the third month, he suddenly

opened his eyes. He was wide-awake. In the pitch-black room he knew he was not alone. He seemed to hear Jesus saying: "My peace I give unto you. Let not your heart be troubled."

He sat up and looked around. His eyes could see nothing but blackness. Yet for the first time in months he knew he was not alone. His heart leaped. He wanted to laugh and sing and greet his Lord out loud. And then familiar words came clearly to his mind in a way they never had before.

" 'Except a kernel of wheat fall into the ground and die,' " he repeated them, " 'it abideth alone. But if it die, it bringeth forth much fruit.' "

He climbed out of the sleeping bag and knelt on the floor. The words and feelings and doubts with which he had lived for months tumbled out of his soul before the living God.

"I'm not afraid to die, O God. Make me strong so that I can trust thee with courage and real faith. Help me to seek only thy will and thy presence each hour and each day. Nothing else matters—freedom or prison, life or death. Only let me be an example of Christian courage and faith. Teach me to be at peace and accept each day as it comes. 'I can do all things through Christ which strengtheneth me'! 'Not my will, but thine, be done. . . .' "

The next morning he took a small piece of paper and the stub of a pencil a guard had given him. Very carefully he printed out the words "Thy will—not mine!" Then he tacked the slip of paper on his cell

210

door at the bottom of the exercise chart which was nailed there.

"Not mine," he said softly. "Not my personal cares. Not this constant thinking about my discomforts. Not my worries about what will happen next. Let my every thought and dream and wish only be to know that Jesus is with me—that God is ruler yet!"

He stood, humbly and joyously looking at the words. He felt ashamed and foolish, and he laughed at himself. For twenty-five years I have called myself a servant of Christ, he thought. And never until now have I known what Jesus really meant. It has taken prison and deadly danger to teach me the way of life!

The guard was surprised and startled when he unlocked the cell door, for Uncle Willie greeted him with a cheery greeting. "Good morning, friend," he said. "The Lord be with you today!"

As he walked down the passageway to the washroom with the guard, he whistled happily "All Hail the Power of Jesus' Name!"

Later, on his way back to his cell with the day's supply of water in his washbasin, he heard the prisoner in the cell next to his whistling too. It was another Christian hymn—"Crown Him with Many Crowns"! While the Chinese guard fumbled with his keys, Uncle Willie joined in with his unknown fellow Christian prisoner, whistling in harmony "The Lamb Upon His Throne."

When he had been locked up in his cell again, he

set the washbasin on the table. He began splashing his face with water as he sang:

> " 'Hark! how the heavenly anthem drowns
>   All music but its own:
> Awake, my soul, and sing
>   Of Him who died for thee,
> And hail him as thy matchless King
>   Through all eternity.' "

That night and morning was the turning point of his life as a prisoner. Through the next fifteen months he recollected in his mind over a hundred hymns, many that he had not sung since he was a boy in his Iowa home. He memorized the Gospel of Luke and the Gospel of John and several of the apostle Paul's letters—before the guards discovered his small New Testament hidden in his sleeping bag and took it away from him.

Before each meal he said grace, even though the guards scowled and threatened to take the food back if he did not stop. In the mornings he was given a glass of milk or a bowl of rice gruel and a piece of bread. Then in the late afternoon they gave him a large bowl of rice, a bowl of soup, and a plate of vegetables—usually onions and leeks. Now and then he got a piece of dog meat or some boiled eel. He did not complain, for his food was better than that of the Chinese prisoners and the guards. After all, as an American he might be useful to the Chinese Communist Government someday.

He had been held in the Yalung Prison for over a year before he was taken for his first session with the officials. One afternoon the guard came to his cell during the midday rest period.

"Come, foreign spy," he ordered, "the time has come for your examination."

Uncle Willie had a sudden feeling of uneasiness. He did not know what they might do to him. But then as he went out the door the words of Jesus that he had memorized from the Gospel of Luke came to his mind like a direct message from his Lord.

"And when they bring you before the rulers and authorities, do not be anxious how or what you are to answer or what you are to say; for the Holy Spirit will teach you in that very hour what you ought to say." He breathed deeply and stood straighter. "What you *ought* to say," he repeated to himself.

The questioning rooms were on the other side of the open court from his cell block. Three guards escorted him across, forcing him to march with eyes front. He wished he could have got just a glimpse of the great mountains surrounding the prison, but it was not allowed.

When Uncle Willie was ushered into the room, he found the official questioner by a desk, going through a pile of papers.

In a moment, the official looked up. "Dr. La-Force," he said courteously, "you are charged with being a foreign agent. We ought to kill you, as we have every right to do."

"It is not true," Uncle Willie replied. "As Christ is my Lord, I've never done anything wrong."

"You are lying, sir," the official replied. "Here is the full report of your treason on the table— everything you have done, every place you have gone in the past twenty-five years."

"Then you know as well as I that my life has been spent in the ministry of healing."

The official looked at him coolly. "Come now, Doctor," he said. "You must be more helpful. We know you sent many reports about China to your capitalist superiors in America. If you wish to be treated fairly, you must be fair with us. We have certain methods to get the truth out of you. But if you will confess your crimes against the people of China and tell us who worked with you, it will save you useless pain."

Uncle Willie could feel the anger welling up in him. But he forced himself to hold back the hot words. "I have never done anything to earn the Chinese people's hate," he said.

"You are a foreign spy!" answered the official. "And we will make you beg to confess. Have you heard of the Wind Tower, Doctor? You are chained to the wall. You never see a living person. The wind groans and whistles without ceasing. Stronger men than you have gone crazy in the Wind Tower. It does not take long—perhaps three or four weeks."

Uncle Willie smiled. "You may chain me for ten years in your Wind Tower, but you will not make me lie. You can kill me by gunfire, sword, or fire, but I will still tell what is true."

"If you confess, you may soon be set free," the official answered. He tapped the pile of papers on the desk. "Would you like to go home, Doctor? Back to Iowa? Back to the cornfields and blue skies, back to your kind of freedom?"

Uncle Willie shook his head. "Not by lies," he answered. "I will depend on God to set me free. You can promise to send me to Hong Kong and buy my passage back to the United States, but I will still tell

you the truth. I am not guilty of any wrong, and you know it!"

The official shrugged his shoulders. "If you insist on being difficult, it is your own affair. You will find that the People's Republic of China can make you die very slowly." He looked up and motioned to the guards by the door. "I am very sorry for you, Doctor."

The guards escorted Uncle Willie back to his cell across the open courtyard.

Three more times in the next four months he was taken out of his cell to be questioned, in a different room before a different official. Then one day in midwinter, he was given a last chance. The official laid some handwritten papers on his desk.

"These are signed confessions from American prisoners, Dr. LaForce," he said. "They give full proof that you were the leader of a group of spies for the decaying United States."

"Don't be a fool," Uncle Willie snorted. "What are you trying to prove? That you have nagged and threatened some poor missionaries into signing some made-up pack of lies? A child could see through these! You cannot change the truth just by wishful thinking, sir!"

"Did you once know a young man whose name was Li-Ting?" the official asked. He looked casually at the doctor.

Uncle Willie's eyes narrowed. "Why?" he asked.

"There was a young man called Li-Ting who used to live in the village of your Tapaing Hospital," the official replied. "Would you care to read the confession he wrote before he was shot?"

"Li-Ting?" gasped the doctor.

"Yes," the official said. "Dr. LaForce, he was fool enough to renounce the truth, and went to babbling about your Christ. He was a traitor to his people." He smiled. "Didn't you know who was in the cell next to yours? You are a poor spy, indeed, Doctor!"

Uncle Willie stared at the official. He could not speak. His fellow prisoner! The one who whistled the Christian hymns every morning for six months!

"But he did not last long in the Wind Tower, Dr. LaForce. He asked to be shot rather than to have to go back to it."

"Li-Ting," whispered Uncle Willie. "My son, Li-Ting."

"You have had your last chance, Doctor," said the official. "Either begin your confession now or you too shall be taken to the tower."

"I am not guilty of anything," Uncle Willie said quietly. "I have nothing to confess. I shall not lie. God never works by lies! 'Except a kernel of wheat fall into the ground and die, it abideth alone. But if it die, it bringeth—' "

"Silence!" snapped the official angrily. "You will have time to prattle at the top of your lungs in the tower! When you wish to sign a confession, we may let you out. The Communist People's Republic of China is always fair, even to its most evil enemies!"

Uncle Willie lay on the floor of the tower cell staring up at the heavy wooden beams of the roof.

"Sins—" he panted, "nailed to the cross—the cross —beams of the cross—"

His unshaven face was gaunt and deeply lined. His staring eyes were sunk deep in their sockets. The wind moaned without ceasing. The whole black cell was full of the wind's sullen howling. It was a living fiend all around him, pulling at his arms and legs, trying to tear him apart. Its moaning wail drummed and drummed at his weary brain. It was like a white-hot iron pressed around his aching head.

"Beams—beams of the cross—" he whispered.

His strained cry of agony mingled with the wind and was drowned in its wail.

"God—God—where are you?"

Was it three days or three months he had listened to the wind? Then in one instant it happened. In the whirling, incessant whine and wail of the moaning wind there came *a new sound!* He listened! It was a whistling noise, yet it was not shrill or piercing, but quiet, peaceful. As he listened, he began to hear a tune.

"Li-Ting!" he gasped. "Li-Ting!"

His heart leaped as he listened to the whistled tune, just as he had heard it the first time—"Crown Him with Many Crowns . . ."!

"Almighty God," he whispered, "am I going out of my mind?" But his spirit was suddenly full of boundless joy. To his amazement the terrifying moan of the wind had changed. It seemed to Uncle Willie like a great choir of thousands of voices singing infinite praise to the living God! The music seemed to come on the wind and fill the whole heavens and the earth with light and glory!

He sat up and leaned against the stone wall of the tower cell in the dark. He listened to the glorious music. His heart was full of awe, for it was a miracle. God had gathered up the wind. He had made its whine into a thing of beauty, a message of the everlasting Kingdom to Uncle Willie's listening, human ears!

And then in the midst of that unearthly beauty of music he again felt the closeness of Jesus' presence.

"Let not your heart be troubled," Uncle Willie heard. "Believe in God. Believe also in me. The wind blows where it wills, and you hear the sound of it, but you do not know whence it comes or whither it goes; so it is with the Spirit. . . . You know him, for he dwells with you, and will be in you. I will not leave you desolate; I will come to you. . . . If a man loves me, my Father will love him, and we will come to him and make our home with him. Peace I leave with you. My peace I give to you. Not as the world gives do I give to you. Let not your heart be troubled, neither let it be afraid. . . ."

Uncle Willie sat there very quietly. The wind seemed to carry the prayers and faith of all his friends in Christ who were thinking of him. The old friends of the Tapaing foothills far away to the east, past the mountains, were still praying for him at this very moment. And the friends of the church at home, surely they knew that he was a prisoner of the Chinese Communists. The closeness of all his friends in Christ swept in upon him. They were as near to him as the living presence of Jesus. In Christ, they were all together.

"O Lord," he whispered, "bless thy people. Hold them true to their love and faith. Help us all to abide in this close fellowship together on earth and in heaven, as we hold fast to thee in quiet trust. The outward work of our hands may slip from our grasp, but thy love never ends. Thanks be to thee, O God, for the victory thou hast given us in our Lord Jesus Christ."

In his mind's eye he saw his Christian friends of Tapaing and the others in America joined by the whole vast multitude of the church of Christ across the earth. He could see them striving in faith for the gospel in a thousand different ways. They used every language spoken by men. But they joined together in the single language of thanksgiving for the love of God in Christ.

" 'Be steadfast, my beloved brethren,' " he said as he sat in the cold darkness of the tower, " 'be steadfast, immovable, always abounding in the work of the Lord, knowing that in the Lord your labor is not in vain. . . .' "

ABOUT THESE STORIES

Here are the answers to some questions you may be asking concerning *when* the stories in this book are supposed to have happened, just what about them is *fact* (since they are fiction), and *how to pronounce* the unfamiliar words.

ā as in ate	a as in sofa	ī as in bite	ŏ as in top
â as in rare	ē as in eve	ĭ as in pin	ōō as in noon
ă as in cat	ĕ as in let	ō as in no	ū as in unit
ä as in far	ẽ as in writer	ô as in or	ŭ as in cut

The Owl and the Cup
Time: About 44 A.D.
Facts: A man named Manaen is referred to in Acts 13:1. Paul, Barnabas, Agrippa, Herod Antipas, Simeon Niger, and Tiberius are mentioned in the Bible. The death of Herod Agrippa is based on Acts 12: 20-23.
Pronunciation:
Manahen (măn′a-hĕn)
Antioch (ăn′tĭ-ŏk)
Barnabas (bär′na-bas)
Agrippa (a-grĭp′a)
Herod Antipas (hĕr′ad ăn′tĭ-păs)
Tiberius (tī-bēr′ĭ-as)
Sacar (sā′kär)
Seleucia (sĭ-lū′shĭ-a)
Caesarea (sĕs-a-rē′a)
Simeon Niger (sĭm′ĭ-an nī′jẽr)

The Fish of Galilee
Time: Soon after 100 A.D.
Facts: The place names are real.
Pronunciation:
Valerian (va-lēr′ĭ-an)
Maxentius (măk-sĕn′shĭ-as)
Corinthian (kō-rĭn′thĭ-an)
Aegean (ĭ-jē′an)
Sidonius (sī-dō′nĭ-as)
Amorgos (a-môr′gas)

Thalon (thā′lŭn)
Andros (ăn′drŏs)

The Martyr Who Lived Again
Time: Between 200–300 A.D.
Facts: Perga was a real place.
Pronunciation:
Lucian (lū′shan)
Salonius (să-lō′nĭ-as)
Perga (pẽr′ga)
Meona (mĭ-ōn′a)
Cosarnum (kō-sär′nŭm)
Padus (pā′das)
Galatia (ga-lā′shĭ-a)

The Death of a God
Time: Early in the eighth century.
Facts: Boniface was a missionary to Germany.
Charles Martel, grandfather of Charlemagne, ruled 715–741.
Thunar was a god of German myth. His name was spelled variously. The sacred oaks, the fire festival, and the Midsummer Eve celebration were real; much that is legendary has become attached to them.
Pronunciation: Boniface (bŏn′ĭ-fās)
Thunar (thōōn′ẽr)
Friedrich (frē′drĭk)
Allain (a-lān′)

Weep No More for Me

Time: Just before or after 1300 A.D.
Facts: Brother Francisco (Francis of
Assisi) and Bernardo were Italian
friars.
Pronunciation:
Nadas (nä'däs)
Pedestro (pĭ-dĕs'trō)
Matrello (mät-rĕl'lō)
Fernando (fĕr-nän'dō)
Estrada (ĕs-trä'thä)
Bernardo (bĕr-när'dō)

Brother Henry and His Bible

Time: Between 1375 and 1400 A.D.
Facts: John Wycliffe, a reformer-
priest, translated the Bible into
English, and sent the Lollards out
to read and teach this Bible to the
people. Sir John Oldcastle, who
defended the Lollards, was exe-
cuted in 1417.
Cawley was east of the Oldcastle
domain.
Gerasene is a Biblical place name,
sometimes spelled Gergesene, or
Gardarene.
Pronunciation:
Cawley (kô'lĭ)
heretic (hĕr'ĕ-tĭk)
Gerasene demoniac (gĕr'a sēn
dĭ-mō'nĭ-ăk)
Wycliffe (wĭk'lĭf)

The Secret Trap

Time: During the spring of 1521 A.D.
Facts: Martin Luther, a German
priest-reformer, was on trial at
Worms, and afterward taken by
his friends into hiding at Wartburg
Castle in the Thuringian Forest
near Eisenach.
The Knight Sternberg was a real
person, but not necessarily the
lord of the castle.
Pronunciation:
Klauffen (klô'fĕn)
Eisenach (ī'zĕ-näk)
Worms (vôrms)
Frederick (frĕd'ĕr-ĭk)
papists (pā-pĭsts)
Hus (hŭs)
Gotha (gō'tä)
Wartburg (värt'bōork)

Liege (lēj)
Thuringian (thĕ-rĭn'jĭ-an)

The Mist at Noon

Time: Early summer of 1559.
Facts: John Knox was a Scottish re-
former.
Lord d'Oysel was a French general.
Pronunciation:
Crail (krāl)
Lairds (lârd)
Angus (ăng'gas)
Guise (gēz)
Falkland (fôk'land)
Cupar (kōo'pĕr)
Lorne (lôrn)
Argyll (är-gĭl')
Lord d'Oysel (d'oi-sĕl)
Perth (pĕrth)
Munross (mŭn-rôs')
Lothian (lō'thĭ-an)

Wild Strawberries

Time: The years 1629–1630.
Facts: The *Arbella* and the *Lion* were
real ships.
The first Massachusetts Bay Colony settlers landed at Plum Cove;
there were wild strawberries there.

All Hail the Power of Jesus' Name

Time: About 1802–1807.
Facts: Rogue's Harbor is a name once
given to Logan County, Kentucky.
Peter Cartwright was a missionary
preacher.
The "haystack meeting" really
happened and Samuel Mills, later
of the American Bible Society, was
there.

The Wind Tower

Time: A period beginning in 1949.
Facts: The story is based on a variety
of actual happenings.
Pronunciation:
Szechwan (sŭ'chwän')
Tapaing (tä'pĭng')
Yangtze (yäng'tsĕ')
Li-Ting (lē'-tĭng')
Chungking (chōong'kĭng')
Yalung (yä'lōong')
Chengtu (chŭng'dōo')
Wenatchee (wĕ-năch'ĭ)